"What Are You After?" She Asked. "What's Your Revenge?"

"Changing you," Aaron answered. "Making you bend to my will, to my way of thinking."

"And what's mine?"

"Getting even with my family."

Talia stared at him. "You'd marry me first. Without your family's approval?"

"Yes."

He heart lurched. There was a part of her itching to be his wife, to reclaim the past, to have what she'd always wanted. Without his family being able to do a damn thing about it.

She glanced at the ring. "This is dangerous, Aaron."

"Do it," he challenged. "Accept my proposal."

What kind of people were they? Him for coming up with this idea and her for even considering it?

Dear Reader,

Do any of you keep journals? Or clock events in your life? I never seem to find the time to keep personal records, but then I realized that I keep track of my life through my books, recalling events that occurred while I wrote them.

During the course of this book, my husband and I moved from Southern California to Central Valley California, bought an older home and remodeled it. What other events occurred? Our nineteen-year-old son, who remained in Orange County, and I visited my sister and her sixteen-year-old son in Oregon and went to the Rolling Stones concert together. My husband's grandmother turned eighty, Christmas and New Year's came and went and our daughter celebrated her twentieth birthday.

A few new pets were acquired, too. My husband brought home a Border collie/Queensland heeler mix, our son purchased a French bulldog and our daughter got a ferret that she named Sid Vicious.

All in all, I've been as busy as the characters I created in this book. I suspect that all of you lead busy lives, too. So I want to thank you for taking the time to read *Marriage of Revenge* and making my wonderfully hectic life part of yours.

Love,

Sheri WhiteFeather

SHERI WHITEFEATHER

MARRIAGE OF REVENGE

TRUNO BRIDES
sk 2

Silhouette®

Desire

Published by Silhouette Books

America's Publisher of Contemporary Romance

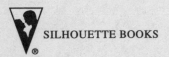

SILHOUETTE BOOKS

ISBN-13: 978-0-373-76751-9
ISBN-10:   0-373-76751-X

MARRIAGE OF REVENGE

Copyright © 2006 by Sheri Henry-WhiteFeather

This edition published by arrangement with Harlequin Books S.A.

® and TM are trademarks of Harlequin Books S.A., used under license.
Trademarks indicated with ® are registered in the United States Patent
and Trademark Office, the Canadian Trade Marks Office and in other
countries.

Visit Silhouette Books at www.eHarlequin.com

Printed in U.S.A.

SHERI WHITEFEATHER

lives in a cowboy community in Central Valley, California. She loves being a writer and credits her husband, Dru, a tribally enrolled member of the Muscogee Creek Nation, for inspiring many of her stories.

Sheri and Dru have two beautiful grown children, a trio of cats and a Border collie/Queensland heeler that will jump straight into your arms.

Sheri's hobbies include decorating with antiques and shopping in thrift stores for jackets from the sixties and seventies, items that mark her interest in vintage Western wear and hippie fringe.

To contact Sheri, learn more about her books and see pictures of her family, visit her Web site at www.sheriwhitefeather.com.

To Dolly Halty and Zena Jeans for the wonderful denims. You made me feel like a star.

One

"I should have fired you a long time ago," Aaron Trueno said to Talia Gibson. He'd loved her. He'd hated her. And deep inside, he knew that he'd screwed her over. But she'd screwed him over, too.

She gave him a confused look. "Why are you going off about the past? Here? Now?" She made a grand gesture at the office they were seated in. "While we're working?"

"Because I felt like it."

She huffed out a breath. "You have no right to blame me."

"Oh, yeah?" He shifted in his chair and glared at her from across his desk. "You're the one who ended it."

"And you're the one who hooked up with Jeannie."

"Yeah, after you called it quits."

"Don't twist the facts." Talia was attired in a designer suit and gold jewelry, with her stiletto-heeled legs crossed, looking as dangerously beautiful as she'd always been. "I gave you your chance, and you married her instead of me."

"My chance?" he snapped, his office closing in on him, even with its floor-to-ceiling windows and spectacular view of Los Angeles. Although he'd made a vow to Jeannie, he'd never really loved her, at least not the way he should have. They'd been divorced for a little over a year, but their marriage had disintegrated soon after their son was born. "It was more like an ultimatum."

"I wanted a commitment."

"By nagging me every time I turned around? By trying to force me to propose?"

"I didn't do that."

"The hell you didn't."

"So that's why you married Jeannie? Because I pressured you and she didn't? Get real, Aaron."

Frustrated, he thought about his ex-wife. "At least Jeannie is remarried now."

"Yes, and to a non-Native man. Imagine that? She found a way to be happy with someone from outside her culture."

"Her husband isn't like you, Talia. He respects her heritage."

Her blue eyes bore into his. "You didn't give me a chance to respect yours."

He stared right back at her. "You and I were together for five years. How much more time did you need?"

"It wasn't a matter of time." When she angled her head, a shimmer of sunlight caught her hair, enhancing the golden color. "It was a matter of principle. You never introduced me to your family."

"You're well acquainted with Thunder," he shot back, referring to his cousin and business partner. "You work for both of us."

"Thunder doesn't count. He isn't a traditional Indian. And neither is Dylan," she added, bringing up Thunder's younger brother.

Aaron didn't respond. What was he supposed to say? That when he was a boy, he'd promised his dying father that he would marry someone from his mother's tribe? Talia knew all of that. She knew what had been expected of him.

Of course that was water under the bridge. Or it should be, he thought. Only Talia still drove him crazy.

He glanced at the file on his desk. They were supposed to be discussing a case. Aaron co-owned SPEC, a company that offered a variety of personal protection and investigative services, and Talia had been his top P.I. for eleven years. During that time, they hadn't allowed their emotions to get in the way. Or so they told themselves. But it was lie, a burden they both had to bear. Every so often, they battled their feelings.

Like today.

Aaron knew he shouldn't have gotten involved with her in the first place. But eleven years ago, when she'd walked into SPEC with her resume, he'd wanted her.

Instantly.

So he'd hired her, intent on seducing her, even though Thunder had warned him that he was treading on perilous ground. Talia wasn't the sort of woman a man could seduce, at least not without repercussions. But Aaron had done it anyway, ignoring his cousin's foreboding advice.

"It was just supposed to be an affair," he said, narrowing his gaze at Talia.

"And it was," she quipped. "Until we were stupid enough to fall in love."

"Yeah, stupid." Aaron frowned. Sometimes he wished he had married her. And other times he cursed himself for giving a damn.

"How's Danny?" she asked, tossing him an emotional curveball by mentioning his son.

"He's fine. He's turning five on Saturday." Aaron paused, throwing her a curveball, too. "Do you want to go to his party?"

She flinched. "I know when his birthday is."

"Of course you do." But that didn't stop her from avoiding the invitation. "Danny still has that fluffy lamb you sent to the hospital."

"He does?" Her expression softened. "I remember how scared you were. Worried about how premature he was."

Aaron nodded, knowing that Talia had prayed for his child. But he didn't want to think about her kindness, not while he'd been married to someone else. Instead he wanted to grab Talia, to bruise her lips with his, to punish her with his passion.

"We should get to work," she said, morphing into business mode.

Aaron couldn't seem to switch gears. He was still thinking about kissing her.

"The Julia Alcott case," she reiterated, reminding him that Julia and her mother, Miriam, had disappeared purposely, running from the loan sharks Miriam had borrowed money from, then neglected to pay.

But what Julia and Miriam didn't know was that the loan sharks had hired a hit man to find them.

And kill them, Aaron thought.

"You're right," he said, forcing himself to think about something other than Talia, to allow the missing women to take precedence in his mind. "We should get to work."

Talia studied her ex-lover, grateful that he'd quit looking at her with a deep-seated hunger in his eyes. She needed to stay focused on her job, not fall prey to the past.

Of course Julia's past was relevant. Talia was anxious to make a break in her case, to do whatever she could to help the FBI locate Julia and Miriam before the unidentified assassin did. "Thunder suggested that we devise an undercover operation."

"He told me that, too."

"Are you okay with it?"

He shrugged. "You and I have always worked well together."

She wanted to disagree, but she couldn't. His comment about firing her had been ludicrous. She and Aaron were cut from the same career-minded cloth. "We'll have to let the FBI know what we come up with. They're the primary law enforcement investigators in this case, and we agreed to share information with them."

"We should concentrate on the personality profiles the feds created on Julia and Miriam." He indicated the file on his desk. "That should help us with the operation."

Talia picked up the folder, but she didn't need to open it. The report had arrived yesterday, and by now she and Aaron had memorized it. "According to this," she said, fingering the manila edge, "Miriam probably convinced Julia to hide out in Nevada so she could sneak off and gamble."

"Yes, but it also states that Julia would probably be wise to her mother's tricks." He took the file from her. "Why don't we start with Gamblers Anonymous and see if Julia talked her mother into attending any meetings."

Talia sat forward in her chair. "I'll get a list of GA locations in Nevada."

"I think we should focus on the open meetings, the ones family and friends can attend. I doubt Julia would trust Miriam to go alone. Who knows? Maybe we'll get lucky and come across Miriam and Julia at a meeting. Or the hit man," he added.

"So this is it," she said. "This is our cover. We can poke around without causing any suspicion. Of course there is a privacy policy."

"To protect the members? We're not going to expose anyone's secrets. Besides, you know how people love to talk. Privacy policy or not, someone will open up about Julia and Miriam if they've been there."

"Especially if the other participants trust us. One of us can pose as a gambler, and the other can be a family member."

"How about spouses?" he asked, snaring her gaze.

"Spouses?" she parroted.

"We can take on the role of a married couple."

Talia forced herself to breathe. "That's not funny, Aaron."

The hunger in his eyes returned. "Do I look as though I'm kidding?"

No, she thought. He looked as though he was capable of seducing her, of making her fall in love with him all over again.

"I don't want to be your wife. Not anymore," she added, memories floating too close to the surface. In spite of his ultimatum claim, there was a time when marrying him *had* been her agenda, the very thing she'd wanted most.

"That's exactly why this cover will work. Our marriage can be in trouble." The hunger got deeper, darker, much more intense. "We can use the chemistry between us. The heat. The anger."

He was right. Their cover would ring true. No one, not even the hit man—if they happened to cross his path—would believe otherwise. "Then you should be the gambler. The one who screwed up our marriage."

"Sure. Why not? I'm good at that." Cynicism sharpened his voice. "Just ask Jeannie. She'll tell you what a lousy husband I was."

"Is that supposed to make me feel better?" At this point, she was doing her damnedest to protect herself. Talia had grown up with a house full of men, with a blue-collar father and three testosterone-pumped brothers. She was used to fighting for her rights. But battling her way out of love was a whole other ball game. "I'd rather not think about what kind of husband you were."

"You better get used to my lousy disposition if you're going to be my undercover wife." He dragged his hand through his hair, pulling a loose strand off his forehead. Aaron had sexy hair, dark and straight and unyieldingly thick.

She frowned at him. Everything about him was sexy, right down to the slashing cheekbones that boasted his heritage. Aaron was from two nations: White Mountain Apache and the Pechanga Band of Luiseño Indians.

He frowned at her, too. "Speaking of marriage…has Thunder mentioned his upcoming wedding to you?"

"Yes, but it's still in the planning stages." Her

mind drifted back to Aaron's wedding and the woman with whom he'd exchanged vows.

Aaron continued to scowl. "I think Thunder is going to ask me to be his best man."

Talia steadied her voice. "I'm not surprised. I think Carrie is going to ask me to be her maid of honor."

"That means we'll be paired up at the ceremony."

She squared her shoulders. "I can handle it."

"Can you, Tai?"

She wanted to kick him. He used to call her Tai when they were in bed, when they were kissing and touching and making each other deliriously crazy. "Of course I can."

"What about Danny's party?"

"What about it?"

"Can you handle that, too?" He reached into the top drawer of his desk and handed her an invitation with a cartoon character on it, announcing his son's fifth birthday, with directions to his ex-wife's house. "Or are you going to refuse to go?"

Although Talia didn't respond, she wondered if Aaron's family would be there, if he was giving her the opportunity to meet them.

She knew it shouldn't matter after all this time.

But it did. Somehow it did.

The following morning, Talia stood at the chopping block counter in her kitchen and poured a cup of coffee. Except for her shoes, the high heels she favored, she was already dressed for the office.

The doorbell sounded and she took the hot drink with her, expecting to see her mail carrier or someone equally nonintrusive.

But she was wrong.

She opened the door and came face-to-face with Aaron.

He didn't say a word. He just gave her an eye roaming once-over.

Talia cursed the shoes she wasn't wearing. At five-one, she was nearly a foot shorter than her former lover. It had never bothered her when they were in bed, when she was sprawled across his lap. But when he stood tall, towering over her with that lord-and-master expression, she fought the intimidation of him being her boss.

"What are you doing here?" she asked.

"Getting a jump on our day." His lips tilted in a smart-aleck smile. "Would you prefer that I came by to jump your bones?"

Yes, Talia thought. She wanted to have sex. She wanted to make him desperate for her, then kick him to the curb, where his hundred-thousand-dollar Porsche was parked. Between the success of SPEC and the financial strength of the Pechanga Band, Aaron was sitting pretty. He divided his time between a sprawling loft in the city and a costly house on tribal land. Not that she'd been privy to his Indian home. He'd never taken her there.

"I should sue you for sexual harassment," she said, finally commenting on his jump-her-bones remark.

"And I should sue you for all of my hot-blooded memories."

"You pursued me, Aaron."

"And you enjoyed every minute of it."

Yes, she'd enjoyed being his lover. But she hadn't enjoyed the longing, the hope, the horrible need to be his wife.

"I could use some coffee," he said.

"Then get it yourself."

"Thanks, I will." He swept past her, making himself comfortable in her cozy kitchen.

Talia followed him. She lived in a two-bedroom house from the 1930s that she'd decorated with retro furniture. She rented it because of its vintage style. The sinks were pedestal, and the doorknobs were crystal.

Chantilly Lace, her favorite Bengal, came into the kitchen and meowed at Aaron.

"Hey, Lacy." He quit pouring his coffee and picked up the cat.

Lacy rubbed her head against his shirt, and Talia wanted to call her pet a traitor. All of her cats had always adored Aaron. He had a sleek, strong, animal-istic charm that drew them near. Them and their babies. Talia bred Bengals, felines that were origi-nally created by crossing a domestic cat with an Asian Leopard Cat, giving the breed a striking re-semblance to their wild ancestor.

"Do you have any kittens?" he asked.

She shook her head. "I sold the last litter. Thunder bought one of them."

"Oh, that's right. He named the poor thing Spot." Aaron stroked a hand over Lacy's leopard-like rosettes. "But what does Thunder know?"

"A lot more than you do."

He raised his eyebrows. "What's that supposed to mean?"

"Nothing." She was enamored of the way Thunder was conducting his life. He'd settled down with the woman he loved and was eagerly awaiting the birth of their child.

Aaron placed Lacy on the floor and glanced at Talia's stocking feet. "Do you have on those thigh-high hose? God, I love those things."

Suddenly she felt naked. More exposed than just being shoeless. "You're annoying me."

"I'm preparing you for the husband-and-wife caper."

"That's what you meant by getting a jump on our day?"

"Yep." He finished pouring his coffee. "We need to get comfortable in a domestic setting again."

"We've never lived together."

"No, but I've spent a lot of time here. That's close enough." He sat at the dining room table, an ancient oak piece that she'd refinished herself. "Why don't you fix me breakfast?"

"Eggs and arsenic?" she offered.

He chuckled. "See? We're married already."

She wasn't about to laugh. "In that case, I want half of everything you own."

"Spoken like a true wife." He sipped his coffee. "I was serious about breakfast."

And she was serious about having sex and kicking him to the curb. Her coffee had already gone cold. As cold as her he-married-another-woman heart. She wondered what he would do if she hiked up her skirt, exposed her thigh-highs and climbed onto his lap.

He would probably love every screw-you stroke. She would do well to keep her urges to herself.

"Come on, Tai, I'm hungry."

Was that a double entendre? She gauged his expression and got a deliberately bland look in return.

Bastard. He'd probably read her mind.

Giving up on her, he began preparing the breakfast he wanted, raiding her fridge and the copper pots she kept above her stove.

Aaron was an enigma, she thought. A city-slick investigator, a traditional Indian and a former Special Operations soldier.

He fixed enough eggs and bacon for both of them. He managed to stay immaculate, too. He didn't get a spatter of grease on his white shirt or gunmetal gray tie.

"Did you compile a list of the Gamblers Anonymous locations in Nevada?" he asked.

"Yes." She considered adding vodka to the orange juice he'd poured. To dull her senses. To keep her from craving him. They used to make love in her cramped kitchen, pressed against the counter, getting hot and wicked.

"You could be a brunette."

She cleared her mind. "What?"

"While we're on the case."

"Why?" she asked, thinking about the dark-haired, dark-skinned woman he'd married.

He moved closer, then lifted a strand of her natural blond hair, letting it trail through his fingers. "Because it would change how you look, and we're going undercover."

His touch made her shiver, right down to the bone. She pulled away, refusing to let him make her weak. "Maybe I'll be a redhead."

He smothered the eggs, his and hers, with grated cheddar and jalapeno-spiked salsa. Then he sat down to eat his food. "That'd be sexy."

She sat at the table too, irritated that he hadn't consulted her about her eggs, even if he knew how she liked them. "A dowdy redhead."

"Fat chance of that." He delved into his breakfast, then changed the subject. "You better show up to the party on Saturday."

"What for?" she challenged, wishing he would let sleeping dogs lie. "We're not a couple anymore."

"Sure we are." He snared her gaze, pinning her in place. "You're my new wife."

Her irritation worsened. "Fake wife."

"I wonder if my family will think you're fake. Or if you'll be able to impress them."

She didn't respond. She knew he was baiting her to attend his son's birthday.

A bait she was sure to take.

Two

Saturday came too soon. Talia climbed in her sports car, a less expensive model than Aaron owned, and drove to Temecula, a vineyard-covered region in Southwest California, where the Pechanga Resort and Casino was located, an enterprise that provided revenues for tribal members.

She passed the impressive resort and followed the directions on the invitation to Jeannie's house, a two-story structure with a white fence and a spray of colorful flowers.

Before Talia removed Danny's gift from the trunk and ventured to the door, she smoothed her chic yet casual ensemble. She'd paired a trendy blouse with designer jeans and chunky-heeled boots that added four inches to her petite frame. She needed to pack a punch today.

She'd never been so nervous.

When she glanced at the other vehicles parked on the street, she noticed Aaron's Porsche. It shined like a silver bullet with its custom wheels and convertible top. Talia's car was black, like the onyx pendant around her neck.

She looked around for Thunder's Hummer, but she didn't see it. Apparently he and Carrie, his lovely fiancée, hadn't arrived yet. The interesting thing about Carrie was that she was also Thunder's ex-wife. They'd been married when they were teenagers, and after an emotional divorce, they'd reunited twenty years later.

Speaking of ex-wives…

She hoped Aaron had warned Jeannie that she was coming. Not that Jeannie wouldn't be a gracious hostess. She and Talia had been uncomfortably polite to each other at first, but after Jeannie had given up on her troubled marriage and left Aaron, the women weren't quite so uncomfortable.

After all, they'd ditched the same man.

Then again, Jeannie had moved on with someone else. Talia rarely dated. Instead she focused on her career. Which could be misinterpreted, she supposed, considering that Aaron was her boss. But she'd stayed at SPEC because remaining there had made her stronger. Seeing Aaron every day, especially while he'd been married to another woman, had shaped Talia into the femme fatale she'd always wanted to be. Of course sometimes she faltered.

Like now, she thought.

Finally, she got her emotions in check and removed Danny's present from her trunk, hoping he was an artistic child. She'd bought him a slew of crayons, markers and kid-inspired paint sets.

She knocked on the door and a fair-haired man answered. He wore a polo-style shirt and slightly faded Levi's. Medium built and casually attractive, he smiled at her.

"I'm Jim," he said. "Jeannie's husband."

"I'm Talia." She smiled, too. He seemed kind and genuine. She'd heard that he was a carpenter. To her, it seemed like an honest profession.

"Aaron told us you were coming."

Thank goodness, she thought. Jim invited her inside, then escorted her to the backyard, where the party was already underway. She took a quick look around and noticed that she and Jim were the only non-Native people there.

Suddenly she wanted to cling to him, but she realized how stupid that was. He was Jeannie's spouse and Danny's stepfather. He wasn't an outsider.

She caught sight of the birthday boy jumping on a trampoline with his friends. She saw Danny every so often at the office. When Aaron, the weekend dad, was swamped with overtime on Friday nights, he brought his son to work, letting him play P.I. at an empty desk.

Jim accepted Danny's present and put it with the rest of the festively wrapped gifts. Then he offered Talia a soda and directed her to a group of tables where the adult guests were gathered, snacking on chips and dip and waiting for the main entrees to be served.

Talia tried to relax, but she couldn't. This party had Indian written all over it. In the center of the grass was a big round object, covered with a blanket. She assumed it was a drum.

Aaron spotted her, and their gazes locked from across the yard. He stood and came toward her with long, deliberate strides. He was dressed in jeans and a T-shirt with the casino logo. By the time he reached her, her heart was pounding. He looked deep and dark and ethnic. His raven-colored hair was combed away from his forehead, and his eyes seemed more black than brown.

No wonder his culture was so foreign to her. Until today, she'd never been remotely close, emotionally or physically, to his Apache or Pechanga roots. He'd never offered to bring her into that part of his life.

"You made it," he said.

"Yes." She clutched the soda Jim had given her. Was this Aaron's attempt to make amends for the past? To draw her into his world? Or was he proving, firsthand, that she didn't belong here? That she would never fit in?

None of the other guests were staring at her, but she could feel their curiosity. An older woman in a brightly colored dress and silver jewelry was scowling. Was she Aaron's mother?

"I can introduce you to everyone," he said.

"I already know Jeannie." She glanced up and saw Aaron's ex-wife coming out of the house and carrying a casserole dish. Jeannie was graced with a noticeable figure and a braid that flowed to the middle of her back. She wasn't classically pretty, not by Anglo standards. But Talia thought she was stunning.

"Jeannie isn't everyone," he said.

She used to be, Talia thought, recalling how envious she had been of the other woman.

Regardless, Jeannie greeted her first. She thanked Talia for coming, and they gazed at each other in a moment of silence.

Then Jim appeared at his wife's side, and Talia realized how hard he must have worked to fit in, to be accepted as Danny's stepfather.

To Talia, it didn't seem worth it. Especially when she met Aaron's family. The scowling woman wasn't his mother. She was his disapproving aunt. His mother was more reserved, offering a proper hello. By no means was she rude. But she didn't make Talia feel welcome, either.

Her name was Roberta, and she looked about sixty, with mildly graying hair, strong features and pale lipstick. At thirty-nine, Aaron was an only child. He'd given Roberta a grandson she adored, but he hadn't been a good husband to the boy's mother. Talia could tell that Roberta wasn't pleased about that. She'd wanted Aaron and Jeannie to stay together forever.

A short while later, Roberta and her sister engaged in a conversation in their Native tongue, and Talia assumed this was commonplace. That most of the people at the party spoke some sort of Indian language.

Aaron sat closer to Talia than he should have. His shoulder kept bumping hers, and she wanted to push him away. He was bandying around Native words, too. Something she'd never heard him do before.

By the time all of the entrées were served by Jeannie and the women in her family, the kids had been rounded up to eat. Aaron led the group in a blessing of thanks, and Talia remained still. Why hadn't he ever prayed in front of her before? Why hadn't he ever blessed the food just the two of them had shared?

Talia picked up her fork. The meal was a combination of Mexican and Native dishes. She ate tamales and enchiladas, with beans and rice on the side. She was curious to try the Native food, but she decided not to indulge, not with Aaron sitting so deliberately close, the heat from his body radiating next to hers.

Finally, Thunder and Carrie arrived. He held his pregnant fiancée's hand and apologized for being late. Then he greeted everyone individually, hugging his relatives and scooping the birthday boy into his arms.

Danny laughed, and Thunder winked at Carrie. They looked incredible together, Talia thought. It didn't matter that she was Anglo. Thunder had always dated non-Native women. But his side of the family was open to mixed relationships. His parents, who lived in Arizona, loved Carrie as if she were their own. Of course, Carrie had a miniscule amount of Cherokee blood. But she wasn't registered with the tribe, so to most Indians, that made her white.

Thunder and Carrie sat at the same table as Aaron and Talia, for which Talia was grateful. Carrie was her ally, a newfound friend. They'd gotten close while the other woman had been struggling to reunite with Thunder.

"It's good to see you," Carrie said, her highlighted hair blowing softly around her face.

"You, too." Talia tried not to let down her guard, to make everyone aware of how much Carrie's presence meant to her. But she sensed that Carrie knew. They'd confided in each other about the men they loved.

Or used to love, Talia corrected in regard to herself. She wouldn't dare feel that way about Aaron again.

After the meal, the gathering turned traditional. Talia was right; the blanketed object was a drum. Aaron uncovered it, and he and a group of men sat in a circle around it and burned a fragrant herb.

A burning bundle of the same herb was passed among the guests, too. "It's sage," Carrie whispered to her. "You can purify yourself with it. Or you can choose not to. No one will be offended."

"Because I'm not one of them?" she whispered back.

Carrie gave her a sympathetic look, and when the

sage came Talia's way, she didn't fan the smoke over herself the way everyone else did. She was too uncomfortable to try to fit in, so she passed the small, yarn-wrapped bundle to the person beside her without participating. Aaron chose that moment to glance up at her. Talia held his gaze for as long as she could. And then he blinked and looked away, as though he shouldn't have been watching her from his sacred spot at the drum.

Soon the men were singing. They started with "Happy Birthday," honoring Aaron's young son with a thumping beat. He grinned like the sweet child he was.

Talia's heart reacted with a maternal ache. She used to imagine having children with Aaron. Danny, with his silky dark hair and warm brown eyes, should have been their little boy.

The songs that followed sounded like chants. Most of the partygoers danced, moving in a rhythmic circle. Thunder and Carrie offered to teach Talia the steps, but she declined, concerned about drawing attention to herself.

When the singers took a break, the cake was served and Danny opened his gifts, with friends and family gathered around him. He thanked everyone, going from guest to guest, doling out hugs. When he embraced Talia, she wanted to cry. But she forced a smile instead, keeping her ache deep inside.

After the singers, including Aaron, returned to the drum, Talia decided it was time for her to leave.

She said goodbye to Thunder, Carrie and Danny, then she thanked Jeannie and Jim for their hospitality. They were gracious, and their kindness made the ache inside her grow even deeper.

When she walked away, she wondered if Aaron was watching her again. She wasn't about to turn around and find out.

Talia left without looking back, even though the sound of his voice and the tribal song he was singing stayed with her.

Long after she went to bed that night.

Aaron didn't bother to knock. On Monday morning, he walked straight into Talia's office, knowing he would tick her off.

With the phone pressed to her ear, she looked up and glared at him. He ignored her polarized expression and sat in a chair that faced her desk. Her office wasn't as upscale as his, but she'd added feminine touches. Pretty dust collectors, he supposed. He'd always been aroused by the ladylike things she kept around. The gun she carried, a pearl-handled pistol, turned him on but good. Not that it should. The snub-nosed .38 was a weapon she would probably like to use on him.

Aaron cringed at the thought, imagining her aiming it at his fly.

She finished her call, and he slid a paper plate covered in aluminum foil toward her.

"What's that?"

"Open it and find out."

"Fine." She lifted a corner of the foil. "Indian food?"

"Fry bread left over from the party."

"If I didn't eat it there, why would I want it now?"

He tore off a chunk and tried to feed it to her. The powdered sugar had caramelized. "Because it's greasy and good."

She waved him away. "Knock it off."

"And you wonder why I didn't marry you. My aunt thought you were a bitch."

"Really?" That got her goat. "Well, I thought she was a bitch, too."

Sometimes she was, but he kept that thought to himself. He ate the piece of fry bread Talia had refused, and she shifted in her chair.

"What did your mother think of me?" she asked.

"She didn't trust you. You're too La Femme Nikita for her tastes."

She flipped her hair. "I try."

"Don't I know." He wanted to make breathless love to her. Today she was wearing a blouse that rivaled the cobalt color of her eyes, and her skirt exposed just the right amount of thigh.

"Why did you invite me, Aaron?"

"To the party?" He caught a glimpse of lacy camisole beneath her blouse. "Because you complained about not meeting my family."

"And now I have."

"Yes, you have." He covered the fry bread. "And it didn't make a difference, did it?"

"Which means what? That you're off the hook for hurting me? Nice try, but life doesn't work that way."

He smiled, keeping it thin and sharp. "You're not over me, Tai."

Her skin almost paled. "You wish."

He argued his point. "If you didn't care about me, you wouldn't be holding a grudge." He picked up a glass figurine from her desk. It was shaped like a butterfly. He traced each fragile wing, memories assaulting his mind. Talia had a tattoo of a butterfly on her bikini line. He'd been with her when she'd gotten it.

"Put that down," she told him.

"Why?"

"So you don't break it."

"I'm being careful."

"You don't know the meaning of the word."

Part of him wanted to shatter the butterfly. Talia hadn't made the slightest effort at the party. She hadn't even tried to make a favorable impression.

He set down the figurine. If he didn't, he *would* break it, snap its delicate wings in half. "Where's the Gamblers Anonymous list?"

She opened a file on her computer. "I hate it when you do that."

"Do what? Change the subject without warning you? Would you rather talk about how not-over-me you are?"

"Go to hell."

As if he hadn't been there already. After Talia

walked out on him, he'd saddled up with Satan too many times to count.

She activated her printer and handed him a copy of the Nevada GA list she'd compiled. "Happy?"

"Are you?" he shot back.

"Ecstatic," she droned. "I can't wait to become your phony wife."

"We're going to sleep in the same room."

"Over my dead body."

"That can be arranged."

"How? Are you going to contract Julia and Miriam's hit man to do me in?"

"If only I could. We don't even know who he is." Suddenly he thought about the person who'd asked them to help the FBI find Julia and Miriam. Thunder's brother, Dylan, was the concerned party. Dylan had inadvertently rescued Julia from a kidnapping just days before she and her mother had disappeared, and now he was tangled up in their lives. Dylan even felt guilty about the assassin, but that was a long story.

"I don't need to hire someone to take you out," Talia said. "I could do it myself."

"Go ahead and try," he retorted. "Better yet, you can do it while we're sharing a room."

"I'm serious about that, Aaron."

"So am I. It's part of our cover."

"Bull."

"If we're going to pull this off, if we're going to become a married couple, then we have to behave accordingly, to get into character, to make our cover believable." He glanced at the fragile butterfly, itching to touch it again, to threaten to break it. "We're not going to blow this, Talia. We're not going to put our lives on the line."

She gave him a cynical look. "No matter how much we want to waste each other?"

Touché, Aaron thought, recalling her pearl-handled gun. "We're going to pose as a couple on vacation in Nevada. I've been working on the details." He paused, explained further. "I've got a makeup man on the payroll who will teach us how to change the way we look, just to be sure that the assassin doesn't recognize us. We don't know who he is, but he might know who we are."

"I don't mind changing my appearance."

He took an unabashed gander at her. "I'm still deciding on the color of your hair."

"Red," she told him.

"We'll see." He wanted to tug her head back, to use her hair to rein her in. "SPEC will provide us with new identities, but I'll make sure the feds approve them."

"How long will we be gone?"

"Two weeks. Three if we need more time. I'll make the travel arrangements."

"I'll be there with wedding bells on." She fluttered her lashes, then mocked him with a breathy seduction. "I can't wait to shack up with my husband."

He didn't appreciate her rotten-tempered wit. He stood and left her office, wanting to choke himself with his tie, right before he strangled her with it.

There was nothing funny about how badly he wanted to check into a hotel with her.

Nothing at all.

Three

Less than a week later, Talia sat next to Aaron on a flight that took them to Reno. Silent, she sipped apple juice and picked at the snack the flight attendant had distributed.

As specified, Aaron had created their cover, right down to her auburn wig. The chin-length hairstyle he'd chosen for her was straight and sleek. The designer clothes he'd suggested were from last season's collection. He'd told her that she was going to play an elegant thirtysomething wife who stood by the man she'd married. Or that was the impression she gave. In truth, she was struggling to hold her emotions together, to remain loyal to a gambler who maxed out their credit cards, drove a car that was beyond his means and insisted on the finest foods and best hotels.

A pretentious Californian, she thought.

The trip to Nevada was the husband's idea. He wanted to hit Reno, Carson City, Las Vegas and Laughlin, sightseeing in between. But his wife had other ideas. Once their vacation was under way, she was going to threaten him with divorce if he didn't get some help.

According to Aaron, they loved each other. Deeply, desperately. So her threat was going to work. But not without a struggle. He didn't want to lose his wife, but he didn't want to admit that he was a compulsive gambler. That he was ill. That his actions were destroying their lives.

Talia glanced at Aaron. He'd changed his appearance, too. He'd added threads of gray to his hair, making him seem a bit older than he was. He'd changed the color of his eyes with greenish-gold contacts and dusted his skin with an amber-hued bronzer, softening the deep, dark tone. Like Talia, his features had been altered with carefully applied prosthetics. Although he still carried an ethnic flair, his heritage wasn't easy to define. To her, he looked like a suntanned American with European roots.

He toasted her with his cocktail, and Talia wished that his non-Native genetics were real. If his culture hadn't been an issue, he would have married her all those years ago. Their relationship would have worked.

After their plane touched down in Reno, Aaron rented a luxury car, which they would use on the remainder of their trip.

His new name was Andy Torres, and hers was Tina. They lived in Los Angeles, and he was a real estate agent who gambled away most of his commissions, chasing his dream to win big and maintain the lifestyle he craved. She ran a successful Internet business, but his losses were cutting into her hard-earned endeavors and putting them deeper in debt.

Once they arrived at the Reno hotel, Talia's nerves kicked in. She was going to spend the next two to three weeks posing as Aaron's wife, sharing rooms with him at night, waking up each morning with the shower running, watching him emerge with a towel wrapped around his waist.

This was too close for comfort, she thought. A job she should have refused. But she wanted to find Julia and her mother. She wanted to help them survive, to turn them over to the FBI for safekeeping.

Julia and Miriam didn't know a hit man had been contracted to kill them. Originally Julia had been kidnapped as a threat, as a means to force Miriam into paying her interest-bearing debt. Only Miriam hadn't complied. After Julia was rescued, she and her daughter had run away.

Then came the hired assassin.

Aaron handed Talia a key card. "We're on the fourth floor. Poolside."

She merely nodded. The hotel was big and

brightly lit, with a maze of slot machines and gaming tables at its disposal.

Her husband, as she was forcing herself to think of him for the sake of their cover, had an anxious gleam in his eye. He looked like the gambler he was supposed to be.

But he wasn't, of course. He was the former lover who'd yanked out her heart, who was reaching for her hand while the busy bellhop tagged their luggage.

She wanted to tell him to leave her alone, but Tina, the wife she was portraying, wouldn't cause a scene in public. So she let him hold her hand.

In the crowded elevator, he lifted it to his lips, brushing it with a barely there kiss.

Gallant, sexy.

Her entire body went warm.

When he smiled, she leaned into his ear and called him a jerk. He kept smiling, as though she'd just whispered something soft and sweet.

Once they were alone in the room, she ripped her hand from his.

"Don't get testy," he said, looking tall and tanned and much too smug.

"Then don't get so affectionate." She fought the sensual chill he'd given her. "Andy doesn't need to be all over his wife."

"Did I tell you that Tina and Andy have a great sex life?" He sat on the edge of the bed and waited for the bellhop. "After they fight, they make love."

"Like we used to?" The solitary bed was a problem, she thought. A major obstacle. "I'll be giving you a pillow and a blanket, and you'll be sleeping on the floor, Romeo."

"No way, Juliet. I'm going to—"

A knock sounded at the door, and Aaron quit talking and answered the summons, allowing the bellhop to enter. He tipped the young man generously, playing his Andy Torres part with ease. Andy wouldn't let anyone at the hotel call him cheap. He wanted the employees to think he was rich.

After the bellhop left, he turned to Talia. "Change into a pretty dress, and we'll haunt the casino. And after I win some money, I'll take you out for a candlelit dinner."

"We're not here to play."

"Andy is."

She narrowed her eyes. "Andy is going to lose his shirt."

"Not tonight. Tonight he feels lucky. Besides, Aaron is a hell of a craps player."

"I'm not interested in a candlelit dinner."

"Yeah, but Tina is. She needs to be close to Andy. She needs to pretend their lives are normal before she threatens to divorce him."

"I'm looking forward to that part. I can't wait to burst Andy's bubble."

"We can fake a fight tomorrow." Aaron unzipped Talia's suitcase and removed a black dress that was stitched in silver, then tossed it to her. "Now be a good girl and get dolled up for your husband. He's going to put on some nice duds, too."

Before he stripped in front of her, she headed for the bathroom to get away from him and slip on her dress, knowing that Andy was going to romance his wife this evening.

And Talia was going to suffer for it.

Aaron *was* a hell of a craps player. Either that or Talia was his lucky charm. Every time it was his turn to roll the dice, he asked her to blow on them. It was cheesy, she thought. But it was working.

They'd been in the casino for hours, and he was racking up a stack of chips. She didn't understand the game, not completely. But it was thrilling to watch him win.

"I told you," he said, dropping a hundred-dollar chip down the front of her dress, where a scooped neckline revealed a hint of cleavage.

Stunned, she felt the cool metal object fall between her breasts and settle in her bra. "A husband shouldn't do that to his wife."

"Even if he's married to Lady Luck?" He pulled her tight against him. Then he kissed her, deep and slow and hot.

She nearly stumbled, even in the medium-heeled pumps she wore. There they were, standing at the craps table, his tongue coaching hers. Suddenly she couldn't think straight. She had no idea what Tina was supposed to do. So she let her husband make a sexual spectacle of her, with other male players cheering him on.

Andy Torres knew exactly what he was doing. Or was it Aaron Trueno? The lines were blurring between real life and the roles they were playing.

He tasted like the whiskey sour he'd drunk, like the intoxication that spilled through her blood.

When he let her go, she knew she was in trouble. That he would con his way into her bed.

But not into her pants, she decided, struggling to come to her senses. "You promised me dinner."

"Now? While I'm winning?"

"Yes." Anything to get him away from the table, from the seduction that was ringing in her ears.

"Women." He laughed, playing his part to perfection. Then he leaned toward her and whispered, "That was some blow job. On the dice," he added, much too softly.

She wanted to punish him, to put him in his place, but she couldn't think of a sharp-tongued reply.

He waited for her to respond, and when she didn't, he touched her cheek. "I love you, Tina."

Talia, she thought, her brain horribly befuddled. *My name is Talia.*

He led her through the casino and into a seafood restaurant on the lobby floor, where he gave the hostess their name and they waited to be seated.

"You're not playing fair," she said.

"Because I'm good at what I do?"

"Yes." The pain of pretending to be his wife hit her

like a fist. She even clenched her stomach to sustain the impact. "I shouldn't have taken this trip with you."

"It's too late now." He rubbed his thumb over the showy diamond she wore, a wedding ring that didn't really belong to her.

She hated that he was staying in character, not missing a beat. Yet he'd managed to speak between the lines, too. To say what he meant.

Everything except the I love you part.

The hostess called their phony last name, and they were escorted to a dimly lit corner. Aaron sat beside her in the cozy booth, and she looked into the greenish-gold color of his eyes, the contact lenses that helped change his appearance.

He studied the changes in her, as well, touching the ends of her hair, treating her wig as though it were real.

"I used to date a blonde who looked a lot like you," he said.

"Then maybe you should have married her."

"She wasn't lucky for me."

"Neither am I."

He reached down the front of her dress and removed the hundred-dollar chip. "Sure you are."

"It was a fluke." Her pulse picked up speed. "I'm not going to blow on the dice again."

He smiled, grazing her with the metal token. "Then what are you going to blow?"

"My temper," she told him, wishing he wasn't so appealing. The candlelight he'd promised was flickering across his skin.

He continued to smile, taking the position of power. "Redheads are supposed to be fiery."

"And blondes are dumb?"

"Not the blonde I knew. She was as sharp as a machete."

"Did she cut you?" she asked, hoping he would say yes.

His smile fell. "Yeah, she sliced me open. Right here." He indicated his heart. "Where it hurts."

Good for her, she thought. *For me.*

Their waitress arrived to take their orders, but they'd forgotten to look at their menus.

"Will you give us a minute?" Aaron asked. His hand was still covering his heart. "We got a little lost. In each other," he added, making Talia's pulse pick up speed again.

Now she knew why Tina was supposed to love him.

Their server left, and by the time she returned, Aaron was ready for another whiskey sour. Talia decided to have one, too. To relive the flavor of his kiss. For Tina.

For the woman who would be threatening to divorce him.

They ordered the same meal, choosing the special, a seafood combination that included poached salmon and baked oysters. When their platters arrived, she adjusted the linen napkin on her lap.

He caught her gaze, looking at her over the rim of his glass. "Do you think they're really an aphrodisiac?"

She knew he meant the oysters. "No." And now she wished she'd ordered something else. She didn't want to talk about foods that made people sexual.

"Too bad." He finished his drink. "Of course you could be wrong."

"I'm not."

"You won't know until after you eat them."

"I've eaten them before."

"Not while you've been sitting so close to me."

He brushed her arm, then reached for his fork, leaving her staring at the oysters on her plate. She wasn't about to put them in her mouth.

"Afraid?" he asked.

Terrified, she thought.

And it only got worse when dinner ended and they went upstairs to their room, where he locked the door.

And waited for her to get ready for bed.

Aaron watched Talia rifle through her suitcase.

She glanced up at him and frowned. "Quit looking at me like that."

"Like what?"

"Like you're going to get lucky."

"I just want to see what you're going to wear to bed." He knew he was making her nervous, and he was enjoying the show.

She squinted at him. "I brought a flannel night-gown."

"Yeah, right. A femme fatale in flannel." He was already hard, thinking about sleeping next to her.

She grabbed a silky garment from her suitcase, and he grinned.

"Get over yourself, Aaron. I wear this when I'm alone. I didn't bring it for you."

"Can I watch you change?"

"No." She removed her wig and threw it at him. Then she released her hair from a nylon cap, letting the blond locks flow free.

He caught the wig. "Are you sure I can't watch you take off your clothes?"

"No." She walked past him and into the bathroom, closing the door with a kiss-my-butt thud.

"Witch," he said to the wig.

"I heard that," Talia called out from behind the door.

"Because you've got bat ears." And a pretty little tattoo that turned him on. He was dying to see her naked, to relish all of those sweet, soft curves.

Talia took forever in the bathroom, but he knew she would. She always soaked in the tub at night. Aaron preferred brisk morning showers.

Finally, she emerged. As expected, she'd removed the prosthetics that altered her features. As for her nightgown, the virgin-fabric clung to her like a mist-veiled ghost. He could see a faint outline of her breasts. "You're not wearing a bra."

"I never wear one to bed."

"I know, but I just wanted to point it out."

"Pervert."

"Listen to you. Miss High-and-Mighty. You liked kissing me earlier."

"Tina liked kissing Andy." The ends of her hair were damp from her bath, and her face was scrubbed clean of makeup, except for her lips. They shimmered with a clear gloss. "But Tina is a fool."

"Don't hide behind her, Talia."

"I'm not."

"Liar." He went into the bathroom to remove his contacts, get rid of his prosthetics and brush his teeth. When he returned, Talia was flipping the remote.

"No chick flicks," he told her.

"I already found one. And I'm watching it."

He cursed and climbed into bed. Or onto the bed. She was stretched out, leaning against a pillow, but she was on top of the quilt, not under it.

She turned to look at him. "Your hair still has gray in it."

"The color is semipermanent."

"It looks natural."

"That's the idea." He wanted to delve into *her* hair, to run his hands through it. "This movie is boring." He stood and started to remove his shirt.

Talia panicked. "What are you doing?"

"Getting undressed." He stripped down to his boxers. "Now move so we can get under the covers."

"No."

"Then I'm changing the channel." He took the remote away from her and found an old western. "Here we go. Politically incorrect entertainment. Check out the Indians. They look like they're wearing Halloween costumes."

"Hollywood didn't know any better then."

"Yes, they did. They just didn't care."

"Then why are you watching it?"

"To annoy you."

"Fine, we can get under the covers. But then we're going back to my movie."

He agreed, and within seconds, they were settled into bed. Like an old married couple, he thought. This wasn't exactly his idea of fun. "I'm going to hold you while you sleep."

"No, you're not."

"Yes, I am."

Talia kicked him under the sheet. "I'll fight you off."

"You'll be asleep. You won't know the difference."

"How exciting for you."

"A man's gotta take what he can get. Besides, you used to like me to hold you."

"That's when I loved you," she said, gazing at the TV as though her life depended on it.

"Then you better start loving me again," he told her, missing the woman she used to be.

Four

After the movie ended, Talia turned off the TV, shut out the light beside the bed and rolled over.

Aaron rolled over too, pressing the front of his body against the back of hers.

"*Aaron.*"

He slipped his arms around her waist. "I don't want to wait until you're asleep."

She gazed at the wall, at the darkness that surrounded her. Being close to him felt good. Too good. He held her gently, the way he'd done hundreds of times before.

When they were lovers.

She shivered, and he nuzzled her hair. "Don't fight it, Tai. Just let it happen."

Let what happen? She didn't want to ache for what they'd lost, to allow her heart to react.

"I refuse to love you, Aaron."

"What about making love to me?" He moved closer. "Do you refuse to do that, too?"

"I might do it out of revenge." Tease him with what he'd been missing, she thought. Then make him yearn for what he would never have again.

"They say revenge is sweet." He breathed against her neck. "God, you smell good. Like lemons or something."

"It's grapefruit."

"They make grapefruit perfume?"

"It's a body wash. A scented soap."

"That liquid stuff?"

"Yes." She squeezed her eyes shut, trying to diminish the power of his touch. The rugged enchantment. The nighttime emotion.

"Open your eyes, Tai."

Damn him. "They are open."

"No, they're not. You always close them when you don't want to face what's happening in your life."

"Nothing is happening. Nothing that matters."

He kept her snug against his body. "Revenge sex isn't nothing. It'll get you in trouble."

She opened her eyes. "You're warning me to be careful?"

"You bet I am."

"I'm not interested in what you have to say about it."

"Because you're afraid of falling in love with me."

"Kiss off, Aaron."

"Not a chance," he said, before he fell asleep, locking her deep within his embrace.

In the morning, Talia awakened to a lilac rose on the pillow beside her.

She sat up and fingered the delicate petals.

When she saw Aaron standing beside the bed in his Andy disguise, she took a deep breath. He'd gone undercover to buy the flower, to bring it back to the room.

"What's this?" She lifted his gift. "An apology for badgering me last night?"

He shook his head. "It's another warning. Purple roses symbolize desire, but they also convey a message to proceed cautiously." He opened the drapes, but he kept the sheers closed, protecting them from prying eyes, even on the fourth floor. "Purple roses represent love at first sight, too. But I've known you too long for that."

At this point, Talia wanted to throw the flower at him. "I can handle revenge sex."

He went over to the counter to make a pot of coffee. "Yeah, right. You'll sleep with me, fall in love, then be mad at both of us because your revenge wasn't so sweet."

Screw him. She threw the rose, and it lost a few petals along the way.

When the slightly battered flower landed at his feet, he glanced up at her. "Nice shot."

"Feel free to step on it."

He picked it up instead, then returned it to the empty pillow. From there, he poured his coffee. "Do you know what I'm hungry for this morning?" he asked, without giving her the chance to respond. "Grapefruit. Do you think they have it on the room service menu?"

Bastard, she thought, wondering if he would hold her tonight, if he would inhale the fragrance of her skin. "Why don't you guzzle my body wash instead?"

He ignored her sarcasm. "When all of this is over, maybe I should marry you for real."

Suddenly her heart lurched, and she hated herself for the girlish blunder. "What for? To make me suffer for the rest of my life?"

"Why not?" he asked, without blinking an eye. "Now do your makeup and put on your wig. It's time to order breakfast and get to work."

Aaron sat across from Talia in their room, gazing out a window that overlooked the pool. While she picked at a blueberry croissant, he devoured the grapefruit he'd been craving, along with a stack of pancakes.

"We need to get the ball rolling on our fight. On the divorce thing," he added, thinking how classy she looked with her stylish red wig and designer clothes. Of course he preferred her as a blonde with stiletto heels and short skirts.

She made a face. "Why do we need to take our roles so seriously? To go this far?"

"Because I need to feel the tension. I need to use the negative energy so I can storm off and gamble the way Andy would do. If we blow our cover, we could blow this case."

"Are you asking me to pick a real fight? Something to upset you?"

"Yep."

"I get to make you mad on purpose?" She sipped her juice, her voice bright. "That actually sounds kind of fun."

He rolled his eyes. "If you sit there looking all happy about it, it's not going to work."

"Fine. How about this? I've had better lovers than you."

"Nice try. But that's impossible." He removed the maraschino cherry from the center of his grapefruit and popped it into his mouth. "You and I are hot together."

She gave it another try. "You lied about marrying me. You wouldn't take me as your wife. Not even to make me suffer."

He angled his head, considering her statement. "At the time I was being tongue-in-cheek, but…"

"But what?"

"Who knows what I'll do. What you'll provoke. And there's a part of me that wants to marry you."

"What part?" she asked. "Your penis?"

He bit back a smile. Trust Talia. "I was referring to my heart."

"You warned me with a rose, and now you're

trying to sweep me off my feet. Is that a tactic for our fight?"

"No, but this is." He looked straight at her, making the most of his admission, of emotions that were sure to implode. "I cheated on Jeannie."

Talia's eyes went dark; her jaw went hard. "That better not be true."

"It isn't. Not completely. But I cheated in my mind. I used to think about you when I was married to her." He paused, glanced at the grapefruit on his plate, at the sugar-sweetened juice pooling over the rind. "But you drove me to it."

"How? By being at the office? By minding my own business? I never encouraged you to notice me when you were with Jeannie." She pushed away from the table, the tension mounting. "I respected your marriage. I was devastated by it, but I respected it."

"What the hell was I supposed to do? I missed you. I missed what we had." He was angry now, too. Angry at her, at himself. "It's the reason Jeannie divorced me."

"You told her how you felt?"

"I was too guilty to keep it a secret."

"So you pitted me against your wife?" She moved about the room, agitated, shooting him vile looks.

He defended his actions, rotten as they were. "If you hadn't left me, I wouldn't have gotten involved with Jeannie. I wouldn't have married her."

"What difference does that make? You weren't planning on marrying me."

"I'm not denying that what I did was wrong."

"No, you're just using me to cleanse your con-science. Get out of here, Aaron."

"Andy," he corrected, even though no one could hear them through the walls. They weren't yelling. They weren't airing their dirty laundry. But the fight was real. The pain was valid.

"Get out!" This time she shouted.

He knew she was kicking Aaron out. But Andy left the room, too. For now, they were one and the same.

He took the elevator to the lobby and charged into the casino to gamble, to lose a slew of money.

For their cover, he thought.

And to punish himself for his mistakes.

Talia waited for three hours, going stir-crazy in the room. Would Tina go looking for her husband? Would she try to find him in the casino?

Maybe, she thought. But at this point, Talia wasn't going chase after Aaron. He'd wanted a fight, and he'd gotten one. So let him live with the conse-quences, with his guilt. If she were Jeannie, she would have castrated him.

The door jarred, and she spun around.

He was back.

"Hey," he said, crossing the threshold, his expres-sion somber.

She didn't respond.

He closed the door. "Are you still mad?"

"What do you think?"

"I gambled recklessly."

"You were reckless with your marriage, too."

"I never said I wasn't."

Suddenly, silence engulfed them, like a yawn in time, a deep, dark hole they couldn't seem to fill.

"Did you ever apologize to Jeannie?"

"Yes." He walked over to the sliding glass door that led to the balcony. When he stepped outside, Talia followed him.

"And?" she pressed.

"And she told me to go to hell and moved on with her life." He turned to look at her, to stare her down. "It twists my gut that I'm not over you."

Talia eased up. She was fighting her attraction to him, too. "I understand." She caught herself before she went too far. "But that doesn't mean I'm forgiving you."

He glanced out at the pool to watch a rambunctious group of kids splash each other. "No, you're pigheaded that way." He shifted his gaze, meeting hers. "But Tina is going to forgive Andy."

She wasn't surprised that Aaron had referred to their cover. No matter how personal this trip seemed, they'd come to Nevada for business. "As long as he stops gambling."

"He will, but not without some slipups along the way." Aaron checked his watch. "We should grab some lunch and get going. The open discussion is at three."

"How does Andy feel about attending his first meeting?"

"He isn't happy about it." He snared her gaze again. "But he loves you too much to lose you."

"He loves Tina," she corrected. "I was never part of the deal."

They left the room and had a buffet lunch, where Talia barely tasted her food. To the outside world, she was a wife worried about holding her marriage together. Inside, the real woman, the single P.I., was getting caught up in Aaron's threat—the lilac-rose warning that she was going to fall in love with him again.

After their meal, he drove to a hospital on 9th Street. The GA meeting was being held in a conference room.

As they walked down the sterile halls, he frowned. "Hospitals creep me out. My dad died in a place like this."

Was he talking about himself? Or about Andy? Both, she thought. According to their cover, Andy's dad was dead, too.

"I'm sorry," she said, recalling the vow Aaron had made to his cancer-stricken father.

"It sticks with you." He stopped at the elevator and pressed the button. "The smell of death."

Or ammonia, she thought, the chemical permeating the air.

Silent, they located the conference room and went inside. On a table in the back, coffee was available. The chairperson, whose name was Kathy, wore an outdated pantsuit and wire-framed glasses. Aaron told her this was his first experience with Gamblers Anonymous, and she welcomed him wholeheartedly. She also gave him a GA booklet.

Once everyone arrived, Talia and Aaron looked around. She cased the room for Miriam and Julia, who may have altered their appearances, but she didn't see them. Aaron kept a careful eye out for anyone who seemed out-of-sync, anyone who could be the hit man.

Kathy led the meeting, offering a message of hope. Talia thought about Julia and Miriam and the threat hovering over their lives.

Aaron, playing his part as the new member, was asked to introduce himself, using his first name and last initial.

Later, the members were given the opportunity to share information about themselves, and Talia waited for Aaron's turn. When Andy T.'s name was called, he admitted that he and his wife were on vacation and she had asked him to get help because their lives were spinning out of control. She was even worried that he might borrow money from unsavory characters—loan sharks—to pay his gambling debts.

Talia waited to see if the loan shark trigger caught anyone's attention. But it didn't.

Once the sharing ended, the meeting wound down and came to a close. Most of the members socialized afterward, gathering around the refreshment table.

Talia approached Cliff, a man whose son was with him. "Are there any other adult children who attend these meetings?" she asked. "Or is your son the only one?"

"Sometimes Lena's children attend," he responded, referring to a bubble-haired blonde. "Stan's oldest daughter tries to come, too," he added, indicating another member. "But sometimes she has to work."

"Is this about how many people normally attend on Fridays?"

Cliff nodded. "We usually have a bigger turnout on Sundays. You should come to that meeting if you're still in town."

"Thank you." She gave him an appreciative smile. "We will."

But it didn't do any good. All of the meetings were a bust. Although Andy, the compulsive gambler, got plenty of support, Talia and Aaron struck out.

As far as they could tell, Julia and Miriam weren't in Reno.

Five

Talia and Aaron struck out in Carson City, too. So they headed to Las Vegas, where the strip greeted them in shimmering lights and opulent architecture.

"I've always loved this place," Aaron said.

Talia glared at him. She rode shotgun in the rental car, irked by his enthusiasm. "I'm sick of casinos."

"You sound like Tina."

"This has nothing to do with her."

"What has nothing to do with her? Your attitude?"

Yes, she thought. Her agitation was pure Talia. "Do you know how many open GA meetings there are in Vegas?"

"A slew," he responded, annoying her even more.

"But what the hell? We'll be needing them. Andy is going to screw up in this town." He gazed out the windshield at the garish hotels, at the nighttime activity. "It's just too tempting."

She squinted at the glaring signs. "Well, hooray for Andy."

"What's really bugging you, Tai? I know damn well it isn't all those GA meetings."

"I'm just tired."

He stopped at a red light. "Bull. You've got that destroy-Aaron look on your face."

"Why do you always think everything is about you?" Even if it was, she thought. But she wasn't about to tell him that his disinterest was making her crazy. He hadn't made a pass at her since that first night in Reno. He hadn't tried to hold her while they slept. He hadn't even forced a public kiss.

She should be glad that he was leaving her alone, but something inside her ached to be touched, to be the object of his desire, to know that he cared.

The past, she thought, was coming back to haunt her.

He kept driving, where the road was packed with other cars.

Finally, they arrived at their hotel. "I booked us a suite," he said.

"Andy and Tina can't afford that."

"Andy thinks they can. He thinks they can spend more on their room since he won't be gambling."

"Andy is warped."

"Come on, give the guy a break. He's struggling with his recovery."

Twenty minutes later, Talia and Aaron were in their suite, luxurious accommodations with a canopy-draped bed, a sunken living room, two televisions and a fully stocked refreshment center.

"Isn't this great?" He poured himself a drink and ignored her.

Enough was enough. "Are you doing this on purpose?"

"Doing what?" He plopped down on the sofa and put his feet up, the ice in his glass clanking, the soda and alcohol mixture bubbling. He'd even tossed in a cherry.

"Acting like you're not turned on by me anymore."

His lips quirked. "Would I do that?"

"Yes, you would." She glanced at the centerpiece on the dining table and noticed that it contained purple roses. "Did you order that special?"

"Who me?" His smile got a little wider.

She picked up a decorative pillow and threw it at him. He laughed and threw it back.

Big, no-account gorilla. She wanted to laugh, too. But she refused to give him the satisfaction of knowing that he'd charmed her. That he'd given her exactly what she needed.

"We should take in a show tonight," he said. "Should I see what tickets are available?"

"Why not?" Suddenly she was in the mood to party. "I'll wear Tina's slinkiest outfit."

"Yeah, we can be the happy couple." He paused to finish his drink. "Until Andy sneaks in some blackjack."

"I don't want to think about that right now." She was tempted to undress in front of him, but she decided to keep him guessing, to let him imagine her in her bra and panties.

"I'll check on those tickets." He went to the entertainment guide, then got lucky and scored some seats to a midnight event they both wanted to see.

Talia changed in the bedroom with the door closed, giving Tina a sultrier look, darkening her eye makeup and wearing ruby-red lipstick. The dress was gold, like her jewelry, like the phony wedding ring on her finger.

"Wow," Aaron said, when she came out of the room and modeled for him.

"I'm still interested in sweet revenge," she told him, finally being honest about her feelings.

"And I'm still interested in watching you fall flat-on-your-face in love with me."

"That isn't going to happen. My getup is about sex. Then kicking you out of bed when it's over."

"Really?" By now he was ready for their date too, dressed in a button-down shirt and dinner jacket. "This I gotta see."

During the show, Aaron behaved himself. But during intermission, while they sipped cocktails at a private table, he caught Talia's attention.

"What are your fantasies?" he asked, his voice low and intimate.

She left a lipstick mark on her glass. "Sexual?"

"What other kinds of fantasies are there?"

A house in the suburbs, she thought. Marriage. Babies. The things he'd refused to give her, the things she'd learned to suppress.

"Well?" he asked, pressing her for her fantasy.

Talia took a long, lethal swig of her drink. "I want to make you hurt for me."

He touched her cheek. "I already am."

When the lights dimmed and the show resumed, he kissed her. Deep and emotional. They were both hurting for each other.

Later that night, they returned to their suite.

Aaron removed his jacket and tossed it over the couch. Talia glanced at the flowers on the table, at the proceed-with-caution roses.

"So?" he said.

"So?" she parroted.

"Are you going to have sex with me?"

"Yes." She discarded her wig. "But Andy and Tina aren't invited."

"Then I guess Talia is going to fall in love."

"Not a chance." She went into the bathroom to remove the makeup that created Tina's features.

Afterward, she stepped out of her dress, baiting Aaron with her curves, with her loose blond hair, with everything that had made him want her eleven years ago. "Now it's your turn. Go get rid of Andy."

He didn't argue. He used the bathroom, and when he emerged, he was Aaron Trueno, the half Apache, half Pechanga Indian who'd broken her heart.

She wanted to kill him.

But she stepped forward and ripped open his shirt instead.

"Damn." He released the air in his lungs. "I really should have married you."

"Shut up." Talia pressed her body against his. She wore silk panties, a push-up bra and a pair of thigh-high hose trimmed in lace.

"I'm going to make you love me," he said, cupping her waist, his eyes dark, his expression intense.

"No, you're not." She raked her nails down his chest, leaving marks in the vicinity of his heart.

"Yes, I am." He scooped her up and carried her to bed.

For a moment, for one crazy instant, she almost wept in his arms. Being this close to him cut bone deep.

"When this case is over, I'm leaving SPEC," she said. "I'm moving on."

"You're going to quit?"

"Yes." Suddenly she knew it was the only thing she could do, the only way to end their twisted bond.

"That's your revenge? To have an affair with me, then walk away for good?"

"I already told you it was."

"You never said anything about leaving SPEC." He frowned at her. "How am I supposed to find someone to replace you?"

"You didn't have any trouble replacing me with a wife."

"That's a low blow."

"Even if it's true?"

He didn't respond, but he retaliated, kissing her soft and slow, removing the thigh-high hose he loved so much.

She found a condom in his pocket and placed it on the nightstand, and when they were naked, he traced the butterfly on her hip.

Gently, she thought. Much too gently.

Talia closed her eyes, but she knew Aaron was watching her. Was he trying to make her vulnerable?

Could she really leave SPEC? Could she survive, not seeing him every day at the office?

Yes, she thought. She had to. The broken pieces of her heart depended on it.

"I won't let you walk away," he said, as if prying into her mind. "I won't let you quit."

She opened her eyes. "I don't want to talk about this now."

"Now is a perfect time."

While they were naked? While he was poised above her?

Trying to distract him, Talia ran her hand down his abs, stumbling over his muscles, over the ripple he worked so hard to maintain.

When she went lower, he sucked in his breath. She closed her fingers around him, stroking him, making him struggle for control.

Frustrated, he grabbed the condom off the nightstand.

"You're not going to win, Tai."

"Yes, I am."

"Like hell." He tore open the packet and sheathed himself. And then he shackled her wrists with his hands, making her his prisoner.

Her emotions went haywire. Even in bed, even in an erotically charged situation, she and Aaron were locked in a battle of wills.

"You're mine," he said.

"Not after this case is over."

He glanced at the diamond, at the fake wedding ring, on her finger. "I'll make you marry me."

Her chest constricted. "Quit saying things like that."

"Even if I mean it this time?"

She broke free of his hold. "I'm over marrying you. It's not what I want anymore." She erased the domestic image that crept into her mind, the dream that had shattered when he'd taken Jeannie as his wife.

"We can have lots of children," he said.

Oh, God. She made a horribly fragile sound, an ache she couldn't seem to control. "You already have a child."

"I want more. I want them with you. Little Indian babies."

"Mixed bloods," she countered, reminding him that she was white, blond and blue-eyed, as Caucasian as a woman could get.

"They'd be registered with my mother's tribe. They'd be Indian."

Anger shot through her veins, like poison, like the venom from a fang-bearing snake. "I wouldn't let our children have anything to do with your family."

"You wouldn't have a choice." He pushed her legs open. And then he entered her. "They'd be my kids, too."

Heaven help her. He felt too good. Too right. Hard and heavy between her thighs. He was deep inside her. "You're a bastard."

"I know." He smoothed her hair away from her face, caressing her cheek. Grazing her. Branding her.

Her breath lodged in her throat. "I won't let you trap me."

"Oh, yeah?" He thrust even deeper, proving that she was already trapped. And then he moved with a carnivorous rhythm, lowering his head to tongue the tips of her nipples, to make them peak under his touch.

Talia gasped, and he switched positions, rolling over and pulling her on top of him.

The canopy over the bed created a romantic setting, but straddling his lap made her feel rough and carnal. She milked him with the kind of heat only desperate lovers could share.

He lifted his hips, meeting her generous strokes. She braced herself for the impact, for the power he wielded over her. Having sex with him, feeling his body take possession of hers, was almost more than she could bear.

A strand of his midnight hair fell across his forehead, and the glow from the bedside lamp highlighted his cheekbones.

How stunning could a man be?

He shifted their position again, so he was on top, so he could look directly into her eyes.

And pierce her soul.

Suddenly Talia wanted to push him away, but she couldn't. He used his fingers between her legs, intensifying the sensation.

She struggled to close her eyes, to not look back at him. But an orgasm was threatening to burst.

When he kissed her, when his tongue tangled with hers, she shivered. Everywhere. All over. Her limbs vibrated. Goose bumps peppered her skin.

She clawed him when she came, and she could tell that he relished the pain, the passion, the marks she left on him.

He came, too. Slick and hard and wind tunnel deep, sweeping her into an erotic tornado.

After it ended, he took her in his arms.

Their bodies were slick with sweat, and the sheet had twisted itself around their legs like an ancient mummy, wrapping them together for all eternity.

Aaron held her close, and Talia blinked through the haze, through the terrifying thought that befuddled her brain.

What if he was right?

What if their affair sucked her in?

What if she fell madly in love with him all over again?

Six

When Talia got out of bed, Aaron sat up and looked at her. Now that the sex was over, she seemed moody and distant.

"Where are you going?" he asked.

"To soak in the tub."

"Not without me." He wasn't about to let her go. If she was struggling with her feelings, with her emotional connection to him, then he was going to make her struggle even more.

Anything to keep her, he thought. To stop her from leaving him—again. At this stage of the game, he really *was* willing to marry her.

She sighed. "I want to bathe alone."

"Too bad." He retrieved a bottle of merlot, two glasses and a tin of gourmet chocolate. Then he followed her to the bathroom, where a luxurious tub and mirrored walls awaited.

She glanced at the wine, at the candy, at the romantic offering. "You're conning me, Aaron."

"I'm being your lover." He poured the wine and placed the glasses on the side of the tub. Then he fed her a truffle.

She made a moaning sound and turned on the faucet. "I love those."

"I know." He'd ordered the candy ahead of time, making sure the refreshment center was stocked with her favorite indulgence.

She pinned up her hair, clipping it with a gold barrette, and climbed into the water. He sat across from her so they could face each other.

"This is the life," he said. "A hotel suite, fine wine and an even finer woman."

She ate another chocolate. "I still think you're conning me."

He drank the merlot. "I want you."

Her leg bumped his. "You just had me."

"I want more than an affair." He angled his head to study her, the slightly smeared eye makeup, the smoky, sultry appeal. "I want to marry you."

She grabbed her wine. "Don't start in about that."

"Why not? It could work. We could make a go of it." He paused. "You could become the kind of woman my family would have to accept."

Suspicious, she scowled at him.

"You could study the Pechanga ways," he went on to say. "You could learn the language, you could prove that—"

She cut him off. "Why you don't give up your heritage instead? Why don't you prove yourself to me?"

Frustrated, he shook his head. "I can't denounce who I am."

"Then don't ask me to do something equally as hard."

Damn it, Aaron thought. At this point, he wished he could let her go, erase her from his life, forget all about her. But he couldn't.

He leaned forward to touch her, to possess her, to try to bring her around. "Tell me you love me, Tai."

She squeezed her eyes shut. "But I don't."

"You will." He smoothed a loose piece of hair, a strand that had escaped the barrette, away from her face.

"This isn't a contest, Aaron."

"Yes, it is. You're threatening to leave me when this case is over, and I'm threatening to make you my wife."

She opened her eyes. "Then tell me that you love me."

Been there, done that, he thought, recalling the pain that had gone with it.

"Tell me," she pressed.

"But I don't," he said, refusing to let his emotions go that far, that deep, that raw. He wasn't about to love her, to get torn apart. "I just want to marry you."

"That makes a heck of a lot of sense."

"It does to me." He needed to wrangle the past, to reclaim the girl he'd lost, the girl who'd walked out on him.

When she frowned, his thoughts intensified. One way or another, he was going to make her his wife, and by the time he won her over, she was going to embrace his culture, his family, everything that was important to him.

"Come back to bed." He took her hand, focusing on the heat, the fire, the protect-his-heart sex. "Let's be together again."

She released a ragged sigh, letting him entice her. "I must be crazy."

He nuzzled her skin, warm and damp from the bath. "Maybe we both are."

They kissed and touched, but it wasn't enough. Aaron wanted more. He spread her legs, then used his tongue, sipping her soft and slow.

She bucked on contact, an electrical charge rippling through her body, making her stomach jump. He buried his face even deeper. She tasted sweet, like the wine they'd both consumed, like the cream inside her favorite candy.

Steeped in sensation, she tugged at his hair.

Erotic girl, he thought. Contest or not, Talia wasn't about to refuse the pleasure.

"You always liked this," he said. "You always got off on it."

"It's just sex." She looked down at him, her eyes turning glassy. "Hot, primal…"

"Touch yourself, Tai. Use your fingers while I do it."

She nearly buckled under his ministrations. "What?"

"It's my fantasy."

"Me touching myself?" She took a shaky breath, her chest rising and falling, her nipples hard and round. "I shouldn't."

"But you will, won't you?"

"Yes," she said, seeming much too dizzy, doing what he asked, what he craved.

Much too aroused, he lowered his head. So he could keep loving her. Tasting her.

Staking his claim.

Sleek and beautiful, she scooted closer, melting from his seduction.

And making him want to marry her even more.

Over the next four days, Talia and Aaron attended GA meetings at various locations, including churches, office buildings and community centers. So far, they hadn't uncovered any information about Miriam or Julia. Nor did they come across anyone they suspected could be the hit man.

After an open therapy discussion at an apartment clubhouse, Talia and Aaron walked along the strip in their Tina and Andy disguises, taking in the nighttime sights, like the vacationing couple they were supposed to be. The spring weather was mild, and the city was brightly lit and charmingly garish.

Aaron hadn't made Andy slip up and gamble, but Talia knew he would.

"The chairperson gave me the name and number of a man who could be my sponsor in Los Angeles," Aaron said, speaking as though he were Andy.

"Really?" Talia responded, playing her part as Tina. They were standing on the corner of a busy intersection with other pedestrians, waiting for the light to change so they could cross the street. "Someone suggested that I attend a Gam-Anon meeting." An organization that offered help to family and friends of gamblers, she thought. A place where they could share their experiences, their emotions, their feelings.

"Are you going to do that?" he asked.

"I think it's a good idea." The light changed, and they crossed the street. They hadn't considered searching for Julia, without her mother, at a Gam-Anon meeting. They'd been focused on the open Gamblers Anonymous meetings instead, which both women could attend.

He reached for her hand, slipping his fingers through hers. "I'm sorry about what I've done to you."

Her heart clenched. Was Andy apologizing to his wife? Or was Aaron expressing his remorse? Was he taking responsibility for the past? For hurting her?

And what about his current marriage proposal?

His determination to turn her into the kind of woman his family would accept?

Talia let go of his hand. She'd asked him to denounce his heritage for her, and he'd refused.

So why should she give in? Why should she have to work so hard to marry him? Study his traditions and speak his mother's language?

She understood that he was deeply rooted to the matriarchal society in which he'd been born. Women in his culture were supposed to be honored and respected. But what about her? The woman whose heart he'd destroyed?

He hadn't given her the same courtesy. There was a time when she would have been willing to blend their worlds, but Aaron had destroyed that part of her, too.

"What's wrong?" he asked.

"Nothing."

"Let me buy you a gift," he said.

She blinked. "What?"

"There." He indicated a jewelry store just a few feet away. "I want to get you something pretty."

"We shouldn't spend the money," she said, pretending they were Tina and Andy.

"Humor me," he told her. "Let me spoil my wife."

I'm not your wife, she thought, as he practically dragged her into the store and browsed the glass cases.

"What about a bracelet?" he said. "Something with our birthstones. Something that ties us together."

Us, she thought. The emotional lovers. According to the profiles Aaron had created, Andy and Tina were born in the same months as Aaron and herself. He wasn't blowing their cover.

"Diamonds and rubies," he said. "That combination shouldn't be too hard to find."

Talia protested, but no one paid her any mind. An older man in a gray suit came forward to assist Aaron in his quest. He explained what he was looking for, and the salesclerk produced several choices. Aaron zeroed in on a classic gold tennis bracelet, featuring round rubies and diamond baguettes.

"This one," he said.

Talia gazed at the glittering jewels. It was stunning. Exactly what she would have picked.

"I'm buying it for you," he said.

She shook her head. "No, you're not."

As usual, he didn't listen. He made the purchase anyway, using Andy's credit card. Talia knew he was going to reimburse SPEC with his own money. The bracelet was from Aaron, not from Andy.

"This isn't right," she said. "I shouldn't let you bulldoze me into accepting a gift."

"Too late. You already did." Meeting her gaze, he fastened it around her wrist. And once they were outside and alone on the street, he grazed her cheek.

"Rubies and diamonds are my parents' birthstones, too," he said.

"They are?" She tried not to shiver from his touch, from the quiet intimacy. "You never told me that before."

"I know. I should have, though. It always struck me

that they shared the same birth months as you and me."
He smiled a little, but it was sad, emotional. "They were
crazy in love. My mom fell apart after he died."

Talia gazed at the jewels on her wrist, wishing his
words hadn't affected her.

Aaron hadn't just given her a connection to
himself; he'd given her a tragic link to his to parents.

To a man and a woman who'd loved…

And lost.

Determined to focus on the case, Talia attended a
Gam-Anon meeting. On Saturday evening she
headed for the designated room in the counseling
building of a medical center, refusing to think about
Aaron's discomfort about being around hospitals.

But as she walked down the sterile halls, she
wondered about his parents, about the death of his
father and the grief of his mother.

Lost in thought, she nearly stumbled into the
Gam-Anon room.

When the chairperson greeted her, she noticed
the usual meeting setup: rows of seats and a refreshment table. She scanned each and every face, looking
for Julia. But the missing woman wasn't there.

Talia sat next to a twentysomething girl with
springy brown hair and big blue eyes. On the other
side of her was a young man who appeared to be her
husband. They were holding hands, and both wore
simple gold bands.

Suddenly Talia felt road-weary. At thirty-five, she

was single and alone. And afraid of falling in love with the wrong man all over again.

The meeting began, and she participated the best she could.

After the discussion, she socialized with the twentysomething couple. Their names were Todd and Katie, and they'd met at a Gam-Anon meeting.

"Our dads are compulsive gamblers," Katie said. "It's what we have in common, what brought us together."

Talia sipped a cup of sweetened coffee. "I'm glad you found each other."

"So are we." The other woman's smile fell. "But things aren't going so well with our dads. Neither of them will get help."

"I'm sorry to hear that."

"Some people won't admit they have a problem. They won't face it." Katie stayed close to her husband. He was lean, lanky and quietly attentive to his outgoing wife.

Talia, playing her part as Tina, talked about herself and Andy. But as the conversation progressed, she realized that she was discussing herself and Aaron, too.

"I've known Andy for eleven years," she said, thinking about the parallels Aaron had created between them and the characters they were portraying. "He's always been the love of my life."

"I can tell." Katie snagged a cookie from the refreshment table. "But I can tell you're hurting, too."

"I don't think we're going to make it." She twisted

the bracelet on the wrist. The diamonds and rubies glinted in the light. Like droplets of blood. Like frozen tears. "There's too much pain between us."

"The gambling," Todd put in.

No, Talia thought. His heritage. The reason he'd refused to marry her the first time around. The reason he was trying to change who she was now.

"We understand," Katie said. "We know what it's like to live with a gambler."

Talia wished she could tell this sweet young couple the truth. But she couldn't. So she focused on the case instead.

"Is there anyone else in this group going through what you and Todd are going through?" she asked Katie, thinking about Julia and Miriam. "Any other adult children whose parents won't get help?"

Katie finished her cookie. "There was this one girl, Janie J., who had a falling out with her mother. Remember her, Todd?"

He nodded. "She was an emotional mess. Like she was on the verge of a breakdown."

Talia's pulse skyrocketed. Was Janie actually Julia? "I used to know someone named Janie," she said, creating a cover, an excuse to pry. "Not that this is her. Of course it is a small world." She sipped her coffee, waited a beat. "When did your Janie attend the meeting?"

"A few months ago." Katie dusted crumbs from her fingers. "She told us that her mom promised to stop gambling, but she never did. Finally, they had a horrible argument and her mother stormed out of their trailer. That's why Janie came here. She needed to be around people who understood."

Talia backpedaled. "They lived in a mobile home?"

"It was travel trailer. An old rental, I guess. Janie said they were hurting for money."

"Did you ever see her again? Did she attend more meetings?"

"No. It was just that one time."

"What did she look like?" Talia asked, then added. "I can't help being curious."

"Because of the Janie you used to know? Wouldn't it be strange if it was her?" Katie paused to answer Talia's original question. "Our Janie looked a little older than me, and her hair was blond. But I could tell it was bleached. Her roots were brown."

Talia nodded. Julia had dark hair.

"She was tall and tan," Katie went on to say. "Feminine but not frilly. More of the outdoorsy type."

"I can't tell if it's the same girl," Talia said, anxious to return to Aaron and tell him that someone who fit Julia's description had surfaced at a Gam-Anon meeting. "But it could be."

Seven

The hotel suite afforded Aaron and Talia a floor-to-ceiling view of the Las Vegas skyline, but their minds were elsewhere.

"How should we proceed?" she asked, seated in the living room with him. "How do we search for Julia and Miriam now?"

"Maybe Tina can get a brainstorm to find Janie and see if it's the girl she used to know. You already used that in your cover."

"Does that mean Tina and her husband will go poking around in trailer parks? Questioning the residents?"

"Why not?" he asked, engrossed in their conversation. "Tina already showed an interest in her at the Gam-Anon meeting."

"We'll have to consult the FBI."

"I'm sure they'll be okay with it."

Talia considered the situation. "I wonder how many trailer parks there are in this town?"

"I don't know. But we're going to find out."

"We can start searching tomorrow."

"That works for me." He shifted in his seat. "I don't think Andy should screw up and gamble again. I think he should buckle down and try to stick with the program."

"It would be easier for Tina if he did."

"Then that's how we'll play it. We'll let Andy prove himself."

Her chest turned tight. Suddenly Andy and Tina had become much too real.

"I think we should make their marriage work," Aaron said.

She glanced at the ring on her finger. "So do I."

"I'm not giving up on us, either." He caught her gaze. "I'm not losing you."

Talia's heartbeat skittered. When he spoke that way, when he seemed honest and sincere and kind, she had to remind herself of their past, of their complicated history.

A reminder that served her well.

"Do you still expect me to prove myself to your family?" she asked.

"Yes," he responded. "It's important to me."

"You didn't marry me last time because I didn't fit your family's ideal. And I still don't fit, so much so, you're trying to change me. That doesn't exactly endear your family to me."

He frowned. "Do you resent them that much?"

"I resent their influence over you." Needing a drink, she went to the refreshment area and made herself a wine spritzer, utilizing the fully stocked bar. "And that makes me resent your culture, too."

"Do you know why my father wanted me to marry someone from my mother's tribe?"

The spritzer exploded in her stomach, bursting into a zillion little bubbles.

Aaron answered his own question. "Because he was influenced by her upbringing. He wasn't raised in a traditional manner, and he struggled with that. So when he met my mom, and she brought him into her world, he found the stability he was looking for."

"And that's what he wanted to instill in you?"

"Yes. He wanted me to practice the old ways, to keep my culture alive, to marry a woman who believed in traditional values."

"What about your uncle?" she said, trying to make sense of the situation. "Thunder's father is fine with the way he was raised."

"I know. Our fathers are brothers, but they're nothing alike. Or *were* nothing alike," he amended, acknowledging that his father was dead and Thunder's was still alive.

"I'm sorry you lost your dad," she said.

"Thank-you." He angled his head to look at her. "I think he would have liked you."

"Me? The femme fatale? Somehow I doubt it."

"I'm not saying that he would have considered you wife material for his son. I'm just saying that he would have liked you."

Suddenly they turned quiet, the city lights shining through the window, creating patterns on the glass.

Shimmering shadows, she thought. Pretty ghosts.

"My family likes you," she said, breaking the silence.

"Your dad and your brothers?" He looked guilty. "Even after I hurt you?"

"I never told them how much it hurt."

"They think you're doing fine without me?"

"Yes." She paused, frowned. "But I am. I am doing fine without you."

"Are you?" Aaron reached for her hand, holding it gently in his. "Make love with me, Tal."

Her knees went wax-melting weak, and she fought for control, losing horribly. When he led her to the bedroom, she went willingly.

He removed her blouse and fingered the lace on her bra. "Damn, you're pretty." He undid the hooks in the back and watched the undergarment fall. "So pretty."

Talia took a quaking breath, and he touched her, rubbing her nipples with his thumbs, making her long for more.

From there, he undressed her all the way.

Completely, she thought.

Taking possession. Giving her naked body chills.

Fully clothed, he climbed on top of her, creating friction, his jeans grazing her thighs.

Lost in sensation, she kissed him, openmouthed and carnal, arching her hips to feel the hardness beneath his zipper.

"Tell me what you want," he whispered.

"You," she said, pulling him closer.

Together, they rolled over the bed, bunching sheets and scattering pillows.

"Why do you want this as badly as I do?" he asked.

"This?" Talia tugged at his pants, pulling them down and rousing the heat, the hunger that drove them. "You mean sex? That's a no-brainer."

"Is it?"

"Yes, it is."

Unconvinced, he challenged her. "I shouldn't read more into it?"

Her heart skipped a nervous beat. "No."

"If you say so." He rubbed her where she ached, where she wanted him, stealing what was left of her breath.

When she closed her eyes, he used his fingers, pushing her into a spine-tingling, blood-pumping, spread-her-legs orgasm.

Dizzy, she let the feeling sweep her under, back and forth, like a siren in the depths of the sea.

After it ended, he tore open his shirt, kicked away his jeans and grabbed a condom. By the time she opened her eyes and looked into his, he was deep inside her.

Thrust full-hilt.

Desperate for each other, they had maniacal sex, moving at a frenzied pace. She climaxed again.

Asking a higher power to save her.

From the man she was trying not to love.

The following day Aaron and Talia searched for Julia and Miriam. The Desert Dream Trailer Park, located on the outskirts of Vegas, was a patch of concrete surrounded by sand.

"Desert Dream?" Aaron said. "More like nightmare."

Talia walked beside him. "It's bad, isn't it?"

He nodded. They'd been going from park to park, where the living conditions varied. Some locations offered a safe, comfortable environment, but the Desert Dream wasn't one of them. "This is it," he said, stopping at an old metal trailer. "This is where the manager lives."

Talia didn't respond, but he figured she was thinking about Julia and Miriam, hoping and praying that they would be able to bring the missing women to safety.

Aaron glanced at a potted plant, a dead fern, beside the wooden steps that led to the door. He wanted to take Talia in his arms and shake some sense into her, to make her agree to marry him, to see things his way. Yet the closer they got to finding

Julia and Miriam, the closer he got to the possibility of losing Talia, the way he'd lost her before.

How twisted was that?

"Ready?" he asked.

She nodded, and he went to the door and knocked.

A gray-haired woman, who appeared to be in her seventies, answered the summons. Her suntanned skin was craggy with hard-living lines, and her dress was an obsolete housecoat she'd probably bought at a thrift store.

"What?" she said, by way of a greeting.

"We were wondering about some people who might be staying here," Aaron said.

"Who?" she asked, giving him, then Talia, a suspicious look.

"A young woman named Janie and her mother."

"Who are they to you?" The trailer park manager lit a cigarette in the doorway, practically blowing smoke in Aaron's face.

He waved his hand, combating her rude behavior. "They're just some people we're concerned about."

She sucked on the cigarette. "I don't need any trouble around here."

Talia stepped forward. "We're not trying to cause any trouble. Our names are Tina and Andy Torres, and we're part of a twelve-step program that Janie…Janie J., was involved in."

"Those twelve-step programs are crap."

"Not to us," Aaron said. "Or to Janie." He squared his shoulders, taking a persistent stand. "Is she here?"

"If you mean that skinny blonde who rented space fifty-one, then no, she ain't. She and her mama stayed for two months then took off with the wind."

Aaron glanced at Talia and she waited for him to continue, to keep asking questions, to take this as far as he could.

He shifted his attention back to the interview. "Did they stiff you with the rent?"

"No. Lots of folks only stay for a short time, whether they bring their own trailer or rent one of ours."

"Did they pay you in cash?"

"Yes."

"Do you have a copy of the rental agreement?"

"Yes, but it's just standard stuff." The old lady narrowed her eyes. "Are you two for real? Or are you bill collectors? Are you hunting that girl down for an outstanding debt?"

"We're for real." As authentic as undercover P.I.s could be. "We're trying to make things easier for Janie and her mother." He paused. "May I see a copy of the rental agreement? It might help us find Janie."

The manager blew another stream of smoke toward him. "I ain't showing you nothing. And don't poke around, bugging my tenants. Folks value their privacy around here."

Because most of them had something to hide, he thought.

"Fine," he said, realizing the FBI would have to take over, flashing their badges and demanding answers.

For Aaron and Talia, it was time to go home.

* * *

It was over, Talia thought, as she sat in her office at SPEC. She and Aaron were no longer portraying Tina and Andy.

She glanced at her finger, from which she'd removed the wedding ring. Of course the bracelet Aaron had given her remained on her wrist, glinting like a what-happens-in-Vegas-stays-in-Vegas reminder.

Two days had passed since they'd left Sin City, and they hadn't told anyone about their affair.

A knock sounded on her open door, and she looked up to find Aaron and his cousin, Dylan. Aside from being Thunder's younger brother, Dylan was the client who'd hired SPEC to help the FBI find Julia.

"Ready for us?" Aaron asked.

"Yes." Talia gestured to the seats that faced her desk. She'd been prepared for this meeting, but when Dylan met her gaze, her lashes fluttered a little. Mostly because he cared so much about Julia, a woman he'd rescued from a kidnapping.

She couldn't help but be impressed.

At twenty-nine, Dylan was tall and leanly muscled, with shoulder length hair and a bad-boy edge that seemed to linger, no matter how much he'd cleaned up his life. As a kid, he was a rebel-rousing hellion. These days, he was a prominent and success-ful horse trainer. He lived in Arizona on a ranch he'd built, but he made frequent trips to California, getting updates on Julia's case.

Aaron frowned at her, and she shrugged. Apparently he'd caught her girlish reaction to his hunk-of-burning hormones cousin. Serves him right, she thought.

Resentment was key to Talia's survival. The emotion that would keep her from doing something stupid.

Like falling in love with Aaron again.

The men took their seats, and she sat back in her chair. Aaron was still frowning at her.

"Well?" Dylan said, impatient for an update.

Aaron filled him in, telling him what they'd uncovered about Julia and her mother.

The younger man made a troubled expression. "What happens now?"

Aaron responded, "The feds already sent a team to Vegas."

"This is driving me crazy." Dylan dragged a hand through his hair. He was dressed in Wrangler Jeans and a denim shirt, looking every bit the horseman he was. "It's taking too damn long to find them."

Talia agreed. "Yes, it is. But that means the hit man is probably having trouble finding them, too."

Dylan refused to relax. "I'm going to Vegas. Maybe if I'm there—"

"You'll see her somewhere," Talia provided.

He nodded, then caught her gaze. "Thanks for caring."

"You're welcome." She considered him, thinking how strangely romantic he was. He would never admit that Julia Alcott had gotten under his skin, but he wouldn't rest until she was safe.

"I care, too," Aaron said, sounding annoyed.

Dylan ignored him. He was still looking at Talia. She wondered how Julia must have felt when he'd rescued her.

Of course she'd disappeared afterward, running away from everyone, including Dylan.

"Do you want SPEC to book your flight?" she asked.

Dylan shook his head. "I'm going to drive to Vegas."

"Let us know when you get there."

"I will." He came to his feet, then stood in the middle of her office, gazing at her and Aaron.

Finally, he addressed his cousin, pushing his buttons, making him deliberately mad, something Dylan was notorious for. "You're sleeping with Talia again."

Aaron all but snarled. "Yeah, so what's it to you?"

"Nothing. I'm just making an observation. But you better not hurt her."

Aaron clammed up, and Dylan said goodbye to Talia. By the time he left, she was grateful that he'd spoken out of turn. That her affair with Aaron was out of the bag.

"He needs to mind his own business," Aaron said.

She raised her eyebrows. "Because he's trying to protect me?"

"More like charm you. I never did trust him, even when he was kid."

She couldn't help but smile. "You're jealous."

"So what if I am?" He leaned across the desk, his dark eyes boring into hers. "You're my lover."

She held her ground, even if her emotions were slipping, even if she wished he would kiss her. "But I'm not going to be your wife."

"Yes, you are. I'm coming by tonight." He paused, punctuating the timbre of his voice. "With a ring."

Eight

Talia nervously waited for Aaron to arrive at her house, his parting words about getting her a ring replaying in her mind. She knew it shouldn't matter. She shouldn't care. The bracelet he'd given her, the birthstones they shared with his parents, hadn't made a difference. She was still the woman he'd refused to marry last time.

Diamonds, or rubies for that matter, weren't necessarily a girl's best friend.

The bell chimed, and she went to the door. Foolish as it was, she wanted to look good for Aaron. So she'd put on a stretchy top that revealed a hint of cleavage and a pair of body-hugging jeans with embroidery on the sides.

"'Evening," he said when she let him in.

"Hi." He was wearing jeans, too. Only his were more casual and well worn.

"Where's my ring?" she asked, unable to quell her curiosity.

He grinned. "I knew you'd be impatient."

"I just want to see it."

"No problem." He reached into his pocket and handed her a small velvet box.

She lifted the lid and sucked in her breath. The heirloom-quality ring featured a cushion-cut diamond, with two round-cut rubies that complemented her bracelet.

"It's incredible." She glanced up at him. "But I'm not going to accept it."

"At least let me speak my piece before you turn me down."

"You're wasting your time," she said, even if she was anxious to hear what he had to say.

"Do you know why I chose this type of diamond?" he asked.

She shook her head.

"Because it was popular over a century ago. The rounded corners and larger facets increase the brilliance under candlelight." He looked into her eyes. "And I've always been fascinated by all the candles you keep around. I like the antiques in your bedroom, too."

She frowned at him. "Don't get romantic on me."

He led her to the living room, where the candles he talked about, scented the air. "I'm not trying to be romantic. This is about revenge."

Stunned, she stared at him.

He expounded. "I want you to embrace my heritage, and you want me to denounce it. So if we get married before that gets settled, one of us will get what we're after and the other will have to compromise."

"So what are you after?" she asked. "What's your revenge?"

"Changing you. Making you bend to my will, to my way of thinking."

"And what's mine?"

"Getting even with my family."

She stared at him again. "You'd marry me first? Without your family's approval?"

"Yes."

Her heart lurched, skipping erratic beats. There was part of her itching to be his wife, to reclaim the past, to have what she'd always wanted. Without his family being able to do a damn thing about it.

She glanced at the ring. "This is dangerous, Aaron."

"Why? Because you want to get back at my family?"

She nodded and sat on the sofa. Her knees were getting weak.

"Then do it," he challenged. "Accept my proposal."

Dear God, she thought. What kind of twisted people were they? Him for coming up with this idea and her for even considering it? "Where would we live?"

"I figured we could buy a place together. Start

fresh. Of course Danny would be part of our lives. He's my son."

Her nerves kicked in again. "I wish he was *our* son. I wish the past had never happened." She paused, took a breath. "What's changed, Aaron? Why are you willing to marry me now?"

"I made a mistake before. I ended up with the wrong girl."

"And now you're willing to marry the right girl? Even though you know that she doesn't want anything to do with your family?"

"Yes." He sat next to her, his presence strong and unyielding. His shoulder bumped hers, making a gruff connection. "But only because things are going to turn out my way."

Her temper flared. "And if they don't?"

"They will. Once we're married, you'll come around."

She wanted to throw the diamond at him. But she didn't. She held the box in a death grip. It was, after all, the ring she'd hungered for all those years ago. "Old wounds run deep."

"Yes, they do. You screwed me over last time, Tai. You walked out on me. You ruined my life."

Likewise, she thought.

At an impasse, they looked at each other, a man and a woman who'd hurt each other desperately. This was beyond dangerous. Beyond logical. Beyond anything she'd ever imagined.

Her head was spinning.

He took the box and removed the ring, slipping it onto her finger, where it made a perfect fit. "Say yes, Talia."

A positive response was already waging a war in her brain, and she hated herself for it. "What kind of ceremony would we have? What kind of vows could we possible take?"

"I figured we could go back to Vegas. Only this time, we'd be ourselves, not Andy and Tina."

"A quickie wedding?" With Andy and Tina's ghosts hovering over them? When he trapped her gaze, she removed the diamond. "Give me some time to think about it."

"All right. But hold onto this." He pressed the ring into her hand, closing her palm around it. "Put it away for safekeeping."

Then he leaned in to kiss her.

To make her head spin even more.

The following day on Talia's lunch break, she strolled along the beach with Carrie, eating paper-wrapped burgers and drinking lemonade. They took the sidewalk that led to a string of quaint little stores, where they window-shopped along the way.

"You must love living here," Talia said.

"I do. I have a good life with Thunder. The sand, the surf, the house where we'll raise our child." Carrie glanced back in the direction of her home. "What more could I want?"

"You and Thunder have come a long way."

"Yes, we have." Carrie stopped walking. Her reddish-brown hair blew across her cheek, and she batted the errant strands away from her face. "Something is going on with you and Aaron, isn't it?"

"He asked me to marry him."

"Oh, my God."

"Don't get too excited. There's a catch." Talia explained the situation, and the other woman merely gaped at her.

"People aren't supposed to get married for revenge."

"Aaron and I aren't most people."

"So you're going to do it?"

"I don't know." Talia frowned at the sea, at the water foaming along the shore. The food had gone heavy in her stomach. "I'm fighting my feelings for him."

"You're worried about falling in love?" Carrie softened her tone. "I'll bet he's fighting his feelings, too."

"Because he's willing to disappoint his family to marry me? He's only doing that because he thinks he can change me."

"Maybe you'll change each other."

"And maybe we'll drive each other over the edge."

"I think you already are." Carrie smiled a little. "But Thunder and I did that, too." She stopped smiling. "Still, we never pegged you and Aaron for getting back together. In fact, we've been concerned about asking you to be the maid of honor and best man at our wedding."

"I know." Talia tossed her empty wrapper in a

nearby trash can. "But honestly, we'd like to stand up for you."

Carrie sipped her lemonade. "Who knows? You might get married before Thunder and I do."

"Wouldn't that be ironic?" The sea rose in an angry wave, and she hoped it wasn't an omen. "Do you really think Aaron is fighting his feelings?"

Carrie nodded. "He's asking you to make a lifelong commitment. To be with him. That adds up to love, whether he knows it or not."

At this stage of the game, Talia couldn't tell; she couldn't gauge Aaron's emotions.

Silent, they kept walking, passing gift shops and surf apparel stores. A light breeze blew, but the water was still rioting, making havoc of the sand.

"You should see the ring he gave me," Talia said.

"Where is it?"

"At home, in my jewelry box. Six years ago I would have melted at his feet for a rock like that."

"Six years ago he married Jeannie."

"Exactly." Talia wondered what Aaron's ex-wife would think of his unconventional proposal. "I don't even know if he's told his family yet."

"He'll have to if you agree to marry him."

"Yes, he will." She watched the turbulent waves, knowing she was on the verge of saying yes and hoping that Carrie was right.

Because if Talia fell in love, she couldn't bear for it to be one-sided.

* * *

Talia returned to the office, intending to talk to Aaron, to give him her answer, but he was gone for the rest of the day, working with a surveillance team on a new case.

Just her luck, she thought. How much more nervous could she be?

By the time her afternoon ended and she went home, she scurried from room to room, feeling like a hamster plotting an escape from its habitat.

Finally, she took a chance and called Aaron on his cell phone, offering to bring some take-out food to his loft.

"I'm still working," he told her. "Can we make it a late dinner?"

She tried to sound casual, even though her pulse was pounding something fierce. "How late?"

"About eight? Eight-thirty?"

Talia agreed, and after they hung up, she waited for nighttime to fall, with her Bengals to keep her company. She thought about her blue-collar father. He always teased her about becoming a regal spinster, a classy cat-lady rattling around with her pricey pets.

Later, she picked up several containers of Chinese food and headed to Aaron's.

When she arrived at his door, he was waiting for her.

"That smells good," he said, about the food. Then he leaned in close. "So do you."

"Thank-you." Her pulse spiked. He nuzzled her neck for a moment, inhaling the fragrance she wore.

He stepped back. "It's not the grapefruit stuff this time. Or the old perfume you used to wear."

She stood in the entryway of his loft. "I'm trying something new. It's called Trouble."

He scanned the length of her, taking in her slim-fitting dress and signature stiletto heels. "Trouble fits you."

"It fits our relationship." She handed him their meal. "I decided to accept your proposal."

He nearly lost his grip, catching the paper bag before it fell. "You're going to marry me?"

"Yes." She swept past him, her shoes echoing through the downtown building. He'd decorated in an art deco style, with black-and-white floors and sharp-edged furniture.

"Why aren't you wearing the ring I gave you?" he asked from behind her.

She turned around, her heartbeat skittering. "I forgot about it."

He was still holding the bag. "You forgot?"

No, she thought. She'd thought long and hard about the ring, but she didn't want to seem too anxious. She was already struggling to breathe.

He gazed at her, his eyes dark and intense. "You better wear it to work tomorrow."

"I will." Needing something to do, something to settle her nerves, she went to his spacious dining room and set the glass-topped table.

He followed her and put the food down. Still keeping busy, she removed a bottle from a metal wine rack, popped the cork and poured two glasses. Then she arranged the Chinese cartons in the center of the table.

"Chopsticks or forks?" she asked.

"Chopsticks." He grabbed a glass of wine and took a swig. "You're not going to change your mind afterward?"

"You mean divorce you?" She sat down to eat, serving herself beef and broccoli, sweet and sour shrimp and steamed rice. "Why would I do that?"

"Because you're notorious for bailing out on me." He studied her. "We're getting a no-divorce prenuptial."

"I don't think there is such a thing." She hid her anxiety with a mouthful of food. She liked that he was determined to keep her. That she wielded that kind of power over him. But she was scared, too. Afraid of the impulsive decision she'd made. Talia had just agreed to marry the man who'd broken her heart.

"We'll invent a no-divorce prenup," he said.

She chewed, swallowed, hoped she didn't get indigestion. "We'll see."

"Damn right we will." He sat down to eat, too, maneuvering the chopsticks like the enigmatic L.A. guy he was. "I'm not losing the game."

She frowned. He wouldn't quit staring at her, wouldn't quit pushing the boundaries of the pact they'd made.

"Stop doing that," she said.

"Doing what? Looking at my fiancée?"

My fiancée. His words, and the possessive way in which he'd said them, slammed straight into her. "Did you tell your family that you proposed to me?"

"Yes."

She fidgeted with a clump of rice. "You did?"

"Yes. And I told them how I proposed, too."

"With a ring and an offer of revenge?" She wasn't surprised that Aaron had been honest with his family. He wasn't prone to lying. "What did they say?"

He went after a piece of shrimp. "You don't want to know."

She raised her eyebrows, paused for effect. "I guess that means they won't be coming to our wedding."

"No, smartie, they won't." He stopped eating. "But it doesn't matter because I don't think anyone should attend."

"What about Thunder and Carrie?"

"They'll understand why I want to elope."

Yes, Talia thought, they would. "Can we at least have an Elvis impersonator as our minister? Something to spice things up?"

His lips quirked. "You're being smart again."

"That's why you love me," she said, waiting for him to react, to sense that she'd meant it as more than a joke.

His smile fell. "That's not funny."

"Carrie thinks you're fighting your feelings."

He didn't respond, but she could see that she'd riled him. Grateful that she'd thrown him off-kilter, she indulged in the wine. He'd already drunk half of his.

"What about next week?" he asked.

"What about it?"

"Can you arrange to have someone watch your cats?"

"What for?"

"So we can go away and get married."

She lost her poise. "That soon?"

"Why not?"

Half of her wine was gone now, too. "What's your hurry?"

"Our wedding night," he responded, his smile returning.

She fought a pheromone chill. Did he have to be so handsome? So hungry-for-her charming? "We can have sex now."

"I'd rather wait," he told her. "I want it to be special. I want to carry you over the threshold and all that."

Talk about getting sucker punched. She clenched her heart to sustain the blow. She wanted a special wedding night, too. "Sexual manipulation isn't fair."

"Since when was this about being fair?"

Since never, she thought. They'd destroyed each other from the start. So why stop now? Making sweet and tender love on their honeymoon wouldn't even the score.

"So?" he asked. "Is this weekend good with you?"

"Yes," she told him, preparing to return to Las Vegas.

And become a Trueno bride.

Nine

Aaron hated to admit that he was nervous. But he was. More nervous than when he'd married Jeannie.

He glanced at Talia. She sat next to him on an ornate bench in the waiting room of the Las Vegas chapel, wearing a classic silk dress with an elegant slit up the side. Her hair was half up and half down, softly curled and embellished with a jeweled comb. On her lap was a bouquet of long-stemmed roses. He'd chosen the flowers, making sure they were purple.

The color that represented caution.

As well as love at first sight.

Had he fallen in love with her on the day they'd

met? At the time, he'd told himself it was lust. But now he wasn't so sure.

Did it matter? That was then and this was now. He wasn't going to lose his heart, not again, not like before. If that meant he was fighting his feelings, then he would just keep fighting them.

Talia was the one who was supposed to fall in love. The roses were for her.

"This is making me antsy," she said.

"Me, too." They were waiting their turn, waiting for the ceremony before theirs to end. "But at least this place looks okay. Some of those other chapels were tacky."

"I still think we should have gone the Elvis impersonator route."

He couldn't help but smile. "You just have a thing for The King."

"Yeah, when he wore black leather."

"I'm wearing black leather." He lifted his feet, showing off his loafers.

"That isn't what I meant."

She shook her head, and he thought about how they'd labored over their clothes: Talia in her glamorous dress, and him in his designer suit.

He admired her profile. "You look gorgeous, Tai."

She turned toward him. "So do you."

"No one would recognize us, would they?" he asked, referring to the people who'd met them as Andy and Tina.

"No, they wouldn't."

He ran a hand through his hair. The gray streaks, the semipermanent dye he'd used, were gone. Of course someday it would happen on its own. "Can you believe we're going to grow old together?"

"Are we?"

"We better." He frowned at her. She'd refused to sign the no-divorce prenup he'd drafted. Not that the damn thing would have held up in court. But that was beside the point. Aaron intended to win the game, to claim his wife and his victory.

She glanced at the clock on the wall, and he checked his pocket for the hundredth time, making sure he hadn't lost the wedding band that went with the engagement ring he'd given her.

And then they both noticed the tall dark man who came through the door.

"Dylan?" Talia said, beating Aaron to the punch. "What are you doing here?"

"Thunder told me you were getting hitched today, and I figured you could use a witness."

Aaron wanted to strangle his cousin. "Well, you figured wrong."

"Hey, I was already in town. And I got dressed up for the occasion, too." He indicated his western finest, which included a black leather vest.

Now Aaron wanted to kill him.

"I'm glad you're here." Talia scooted over, offering Dylan a seat on the bench.

"Thanks." The younger man grinned and parked his butt on the other side of Aaron's soon-to-be wife.

So there they were, the three of them.

Aaron leaned over. "I'm going to crash your wedding someday. And I'm going to flirt with your bride, too."

"If you do, Talia will shoot you. Besides, I'm not the marrying type."

"Neither is Aaron," Talia quipped.

"I am now." He grabbed her hand and held it, nearly knocking her bouquet onto the floor.

"Careful," Dylan said, his voice turning serious.

Aaron studied his cousin, unsure of what to make of him. Dylan's life was as mixed up as Aaron and Talia's. The woman he'd come to Las Vegas to find was still missing.

A few minutes later, the minister appeared, and soon the ceremony was underway.

An older lady played the song they'd chosen, and Aaron stood at the altar and watched Talia walk down the aisle.

Candles lit her way and a stained glass window caught the late-day sun, creating a prism of color.

When she stood next to him, he looked into her eyes, anxious to say his vows. And when his time came, he repeated the words carefully and placed the ring he'd been obsessing about on her finger.

She gave him a wedding band, too, and the weight of it felt good on his hand.

Finally, he kissed her, and they were husband and wife. Just like that, he'd married the girl he'd lost.

Afterward, Dylan hugged them, and Aaron could tell that his cousin was being sincere.

"Take care of her," Dylan whispered.

"I will," Aaron whispered back. "I swear, I will."

Talia and Aaron shared a quiet dinner at a fine-dining restaurant in their hotel, then took the elevator to their room. They were staying in a honeymoon suite on the top floor.

He unlocked the door and scooped her into his arms, carrying her over the threshold, just as he'd promised he would. She kissed him, nearly making him stumble. He laughed and swung her in a circle.

And at that simple moment, Talia knew that she loved him. That she'd fallen head over heels again. Only this time he was her husband.

Oh, God, she thought, fear pulsing through her veins.

He set her on her feet, and she told herself to stay calm, to not worry about the galloping cadence of her heart. She was still going to fight to win the game.

"What do you think of our accommodations?" he asked.

She blinked, looked around, saw that the suite was a romantic paradise: a cozy kitchen, a glamorous sitting area, a boudoir-style bedroom and a gracefully tiled bathroom with a garden-setting hot tub.

"There's champagne on ice," he said. "And dessert." He took her hand, leading her farther into the bedroom.

He'd ordered a two-tiered wedding cake decorated with white icing and edible beads that formed a colorful American Indian design.

"You cheated," she said, thinking how disturbingly beautiful it was. A cultural ploy, she thought. A reminder that she'd just married a Native man.

He ignored her comment and lit several tall white candles, creating an even softer ambience.

When Talia took a closer look at the cake, she noticed there were butterflies in the beaded design.

He popped the cork on the champagne, and the sound shot through her like a handgun blast.

He'd cheated but good.

"Here's to us," he said.

She accepted a flute of champagne, lifting it in a toast. She wasn't about to let him win. "To revenge."

That made him smile. "Mine."

"And mine." She clanked his glass, and the crystal chimed between them.

He set down his drink, removed his tie, then took off his jacket, tossing them onto the back of a chair. The rose in his lapel, which matched the flowers in her bouquet, came unpinned and fell to the floor.

"Should we cut the cake?" he asked.

She nodded, wanting to fill her senses with something sweet. The champagne had already gone to her head. Or was it Aaron?

He handed her a ribbon-wrapped knife. "You can have the honor."

She angled the blade. "You actually trust me with this?"

"I've been cut before." He looked into her eyes. "Bone deep."

Yes, she thought. She'd hurt him before. And he'd hurt her, too. Yet they'd gotten married anyway.

Silent, Talia sliced into the bottom layer of the cake, discovering banana-cream filling.

"There's a mirror above the bed," he said.

She looked up and felt her skin tingle. "It's a hotel cliché. What newlyweds expect."

"Yeah." He finished his champagne. "Honeymoon suites are supposed to be romantic."

"Or decadent." She handed him a piece of cake, a fork and a linen napkin. He sat on the edge of the bed to eat it. She joined him with her plate, and they tasted the delectable treat.

But within no time, his mind strayed. "Let me undress you, Tai."

Her heart hit her chest. "What about dessert?"

"I'd rather have you." He took his cake, and then hers, placing them on the nightstand.

Unable to resist, she moved closer, and he worked the zipper on her dress. Beneath the white silk, she wore matching lingerie, thigh-high stockings and a garter that fit provocatively around her thigh.

"You look like a bride," he said, as though mesmerized by the femininity of it all.

"I was tempted to put my gun in the garter."

"That would have done me in." He kissed her deep and slow. "Lethal women turn me on."

"I know." But it was a proper wife his family

wanted him to have. "It's my turn to undress you." She stripped him down to his boxers, running her hands along his skin, arousing him with her touch, with the passion brimming between them.

Once they were in bed, with the covers pushed out of the way, they removed their undergarments, revealing their nakedness.

And the primal urges that went with it.

He enticed her, making her ache, making her yearn for him. Her former lover, she thought. Her brand-new husband.

Together, they went erotically mad. He slid down her body, and she shifted positions and did the same thing to him.

He fisted her hair while she took him in her mouth, and she rocked against his tongue, letting him taste her.

Talia climaxed hard and fast, shuddering in naughty waves, loving every slick, hot-blooded sensation. Aaron pulled away before it happened to him.

After they separated, his chest rose and fell. So did hers. Both were breathing heavily.

"Why didn't you let me finish it for you?" she finally asked.

"Because I want to come inside you." He turned to face her, to trail a finger along her skin. "And I want to watch."

She shivered, feeling like a bad-girl bride. "You want me to be on top?"

He nodded, and she straddled his lap, making him murmur something rough, something sexy.

They utilized a condom, and she rode him, taking him deep, letting him gaze up at the mirror. She arched her body so he could see where they were joined, so he could enjoy every carnal detail.

"Don't ever leave me," he said, gripping her waist.

She didn't respond, and he lunged forward to drag her even closer.

"Promise." He grazed the side of her neck, using his teeth, nipping her the way a stallion does to a mare. "Promise you won't leave."

She couldn't. Even if she'd taken a sacred vow.

He refused to let go. "Divorce isn't an option."

"Isn't it?" Her pulse hammered to a ragged beat. "What if we fail?"

"What are you talking about?"

"You keep saying that one of us will win. But what if we both lose? What if neither of us gives in?"

"Don't talk like that. Not tonight." He rolled over, pinning her beneath him. "Look up. Look how right we are for each other."

She did what he told her to do, and the images in the mirror made her catch her breath: his copper skin, her pale blonde hair.

When she shifted her gaze, their eyes met. She didn't even consider telling him that she loved him. Because she knew it would weaken her chance of surviving the emotional warfare. So she made love with him instead.

Losing herself in his touch.

In being his wife.

* * *

The following morning Aaron got up and put on his robe, intending to get some breakfast. Talia was still asleep, with the mirror above the bed reminding him of the sex-tousled night they'd had.

His skin went warm.

Much too warm.

Suddenly his cell phone rang.

He grabbed the chiming device and went into the living room, barely hearing the voice on the other end of the line. Then he realized it was a federal agent.

He snapped to attention.

"I have some information," the other man said.

Aaron listened, troubled by what he'd learned. When the call ended, he went into the kitchen to pour some orange juice and retrieve a shrink-wrapped basket of croissants, muffins and bagels the hotel had provided. He added disposable packets of cream cheese, jelly and butter, compliments of the hotel, as well.

He carried the simple breakfast into the bedroom, sat in an overstuffed chair and waited for Talia to rouse. She didn't stir right away, so he watched her sleep, thinking how soft and sultry she looked. Part of her hair was draped across her face, creating a Veronica Lake, 1940s-pinup-girl effect.

Finally her lashes fluttered and she opened her eyes. Groggy, she moved her hair out of the way and the peek-a-boo look vanished. Only now the sheet had slipped, exposing a portion of her breasts.

Aaron wanted to climb back into bed with her, to make long, lazy love, but he offered her a glass of orange juice instead.

"Vitamin C," he said.

She glanced at the basket. "And starch and sugar. Can I have a blueberry muffin? I'm ravenous."

So was he. They'd had a hell of a honeymoon, doing wicked things to each other for half the night. He unwrapped the basket and handed her the muffin.

She thanked him and set it on the nightstand with her orange juice. Then she pulled a tank top over her head and slipped on a pair of panties. Sitting on the edge of the bed, she began to eat.

He went after a bagel and cream cheese, and without the benefit of napkins, they curbed their hunger, spilling crumbs in the process. He waited until she was on her second helping before he destroyed their morning-after intimacy. "An agent called while you were asleep."

"Why?" Concern edged her voice. "What happened?"

"Miriam is dead."

"Oh, God." Her skin paled. "The hit man?"

"Yes. But he was caught, and he's willing to testify against the loan sharks who hired him if the feds will cut him a deal. He'll testify as long as they assign him to protective custody. He knows he would never survive prison without it, not as a hit man turned snitch."

"What about Julia?" Talia asked. "What happened to her?"

"Nothing. According to the federal investigation, Miriam and Julia had a falling out and parted ways, so Julia wasn't with her when she got shot." He saw the relief in Talia's eyes and reached out to touch her hand. "The hit man couldn't find Julia, so she's safe now. Wherever she is."

"I'm so glad she survived." Talia sighed. "But someone still needs to locate her, to tell her what happened to Miriam."

"We'll discuss it with Dylan. He's our client. He hired us to work on this case."

"Yes, of course."

When silence engulfed the room, Aaron studied his wife. "Why don't you ever talk about your mom?"

She started. "What? Why are you bringing this up now?"

"Because what happened to Miriam got me thinking."

"I don't see the correlation. Julia's mom was murdered and mine had a heart attack."

"Death is death." His voice was somber. "Besides you've never told me anything specific about your mom, other than she died when you were young. You've never even showed me her picture."

When she didn't respond, he pushed the issue. "I know darn well that losing your mom impacted your life. And now I want to get closer to you, to feel what you're feeling."

"Because we're married?" she asked, looking uncomfortable, cautious, complex.

"Yes." Somehow the eleven years that they'd been acquainted didn't seem like enough.

In some ways, he and Talia didn't know each other at all.

Ten

Talia wasn't ready to talk about her mother, to expose that side of her heart, to open up to Aaron. Because she was afraid, she thought. Afraid of giving him too much.

Then losing it all.

So she and Aaron behaved awkwardly, the tension between them palpable. They bathed, but not together. She soaked in the tub, and he used the shower. Afterward, he went into the bedroom.

Struggling with self-imposed loneliness, Talia stood at the sink and put the finishing touches on her makeup.

By the time she entered the bedroom, Aaron had donned jeans and a button-down shirt that he hadn't bothered to tuck in.

Avoiding his gaze, Talia removed her robe and got dressed, putting on a pair of white slacks and a blue T-shirt with a jeweled neckline.

He glanced up, breaking the silence. "That matches your eyes."

"My top?"

He nodded. "I've always liked your eyes."

"Thank-you." Suddenly she wanted to cuddle in his arms, but she fussed with a pair of slingback heels instead.

He angled his head, something he always he did when he analyzed her. "Did you tell your dad about us?"

"About our wedding?" The shoes made her taller, giving her a false sense of height. "Not yet."

"What do you think he'll say?" Aaron frowned a little. "Will he be disappointed that we didn't have a big ceremony? That he didn't get to give you away?"

"He'll understand."

"Are you sure?"

"Yes. My parents eloped, too."

"Really?" Aaron pondered what she'd told him. "Then I guess it's okay."

"Yes, it is." When the silence stretched between them, she changed the subject. "We should call Dylan and tell him about Miriam."

"I already did. He's meeting us downstairs."

"Where?"

"At the main casino bar." Aaron checked his watch. "In about thirty minutes."

"We might as well go early." She couldn't take being cooped up in their suite, no matter how luxurious it was.

"Don't be upset, Tai."

"I'm just scared." She moved closer. "Like I was last night." Of loving him, she thought. Of losing him. Of not being able to make their marriage work.

He took her in his arms. "It'll be okay. I swear it will."

She clung to him a little too tightly, a little too hard. How could he make promises he couldn't keep?

"Will you gamble with me later?" he asked, trying to lighten her mood, to ease the tension he must have felt in her body. "Will you blow on the dice?"

She gave him a behave-yourself nudge, and he laughed.

"I like being your husband." He kissed her, and she tasted his toothpaste, the mint-fresh flavor that lingered.

"And I like being your wife." But for Talia, that created even more fear, more worries. If their marriage fell apart, if their vows faltered, she would be left with bittersweet memories, with days like today.

When they left the suite, she grabbed her purse and slung it over her arm. Aaron held her hand, keeping her within his reach, encouraging her to relax.

The casino bar was dimly lit, with the sights and sounds of slot machines zinging all around it. Aaron and Talia took a secluded table, ordering soft drinks, chicken wings and artichoke dip to combat the quickie breakfast they'd had.

After the food arrived, she went for the dip. It was

served with chunks of bread, chips and raw vegetables, making it a hearty snack.

"We can hit the buffet later," he said.

She smiled, caught up in the moment. "All we do is eat."

"We're going to gamble, too." He leaned in close. "Then go back to our room and make love. I haven't gotten my fill of you yet."

"Me, neither," she told him, sounding like the newlywed she was.

Five minutes later, Dylan showed up with a grim expression, and Talia felt guilty for enjoying herself.

"I'm sorry," he told her, as he sat down. "I don't mean to spoil this for you."

"It's okay," she responded, impressed by how perceptive he was. "We're concerned about Julia, too."

Dylan waved away the waitress when she approached to take his order. Apparently he wasn't interested in food or drink.

"Do you think she's still in Vegas?" he asked Aaron.

"In Nevada, yes, in Vegas, no. She probably left after she and Miriam parted ways."

"And now Miriam is dead." Dylan frowned. "Any ideas where Julia might be?"

"You can talk to the fed's profiler about that." Aaron lifted his soda and took a drink. "They're willing to work with you on this. They know you feel responsible for her."

"I so damned relieved that Julia is safe," Dylan said. "But this isn't over for me. Not until I find her."

Because she consumed him, Talia thought. Julia Alcott had become his obsession, his entire world.

And Talia knew how dangerous that was. She was going home to live with Aaron.

When the Vegas honeymoon ended, Talia and Aaron returned to Los Angeles. Only home was a different environment for Talia. She gave a thirty-day notice on her rental house, packed up her belongings, including her cats and moved in with Aaron. She put some of her furniture in storage and began redecorating his loft with the rest, merging his style with hers.

"Is this going to work?" he asked, as he made room for an armoire.

She studied the spacious bedroom. She loved the industrial floors and luxurious skylights. "It'll look great when we're done."

"I think we should contact a Realtor and start shopping for a house soon."

She walked over to her antique vanity and arranged perfumes, lotions and pastel-colored candles. "Are you planning on selling this place?"

He came up behind her. "I haven't decided."

"What about your other house?" The one on tribal lands, she thought. "Do you spend much time there?"

"I try to." He caught her gaze in the mirror. "Mostly on holidays and special occasions. And now I'll be doing that with you."

Yes, she thought. With his wife.

Talia was tempted to tell him that she loved him, but she was afraid to say the words out loud. To give in. To let go.

Because she wanted him to compromise, too.

Aaron broke eye contact. "Did you call your dad yet? Did you tell him about us?"

She nodded. She'd phoned him this morning. "He seemed pleased. Shocked, but pleased. He always wanted us to stay together." Her father and her brothers were men's men, and Aaron was just what they'd envisioned for her. Which made her feelings about his family even more difficult. If she tried to win their affection and they rejected her, things would only get worse.

"We should invite your dad over," he said. "Your brothers, too."

"That'd be nice. They'd like that."

She put her jewelry box on his dresser and her stilettos in his closet. He sat on the edge of the bed and watched her.

"How about tomorrow?" he asked.

"For what?"

"To have your dad and your brothers over. I've got Danny this weekend. We can introduce them."

"I'm looking forward to seeing Danny." She paused, thinking about how sweet Aaron's little boy was. "He's going to be the only kid in my family." All of her brothers were divorced, but none of them had children.

Aaron pulled his hair away from his face. He was

dressed in grungy clothes and a pair of steel-toed boots, looking as rough and rugged as her blue-collar brothers. But he'd been moving furniture today.

"There'll be more," he said.

"More what?"

"More kids." He gave her a half-cocked smile. "When I get you pregnant."

Her stomach fluttered. "It's too soon. We can't…not now…not…"

"Not what? Before we know if we're going to make it? I already told you, Tai. I'm not letting you go. You're in for the long haul."

She wanted to have children with him, to carry his babies in her womb. But she needed more time.

"You'd be good mom," he said, making her heart catch in her throat.

"Thank-you. But that doesn't mean I'm ready."

He frowned, angled his head, analyzed her. "Was your mom a good mom?"

Her heart remained in her throat, beating at the pulse of her neck. "Yes, very much."

"Tell me about her, Tai."

She made a show of seeming busy. "Now? While I'm in the middle of unpacking?"

"There isn't much left to do. And you brought your photo albums." He pointed to a plastic bin she'd put in the closet. "That's what's in there, isn't it?"

Talia nodded. She knew it was foolish to hide her emotions from him, to pretend that a part of her hadn't died with her mother.

"Then let me look through them. Share your childhood with me."

She agreed, and they went outside, where a rooftop patio presented a stunning view of the city. They sat at a tile-topped table near a stone firepit he used in the winter.

Talia flipped the top on the plastic bin and removed the photo album that contained images of her mother. She opened the first page. "I don't have that many pictures of her. Dad kept most of them."

"Is this her?" Aaron asked.

"Yes." Talia looked at the photograph in question. Her mother was blond, with long straight hair, a slim black dress and smoky blue eyes.

"She was beautiful." He glanced up. "Glamorous. Like you."

"I wanted to be like her when I grew up. I used to watch her getting ready for work, putting on her makeup, checking her appearance in the mirror."

"It's where you got the femme fatale thing. I hadn't expected that."

She turned the page. "Gayle Gibson was a nightclub singer."

He studied the next picture, which was even more elegant than the last. "Is that how your dad met her? Did he see her in a club?"

"No." Talia smiled a little. "She was an Iowa farm girl when they got together, dreaming of Hollywood. My dad brought her to L.A."

Aaron smiled, too. "Before or after they eloped?"

"After. They rented an apartment on Franklin Avenue, and he got a job as a plumber, which was what he'd been doing in Iowa."

"So they moved to California and had four kids while she worked on her career?"

"Yes, but she was always there for us. Packing our lunches, sending us off to school, helping us with our homework before she got dolled up and went to work."

He gazed into her eyes, as if he were gazing into her soul. "I'm sorry you lost her, Tai."

She wanted to cry, but she couldn't bear to break down in front of him. "I was twelve when she died. A skinny, gangly girl who was left with three rowdy brothers and a dad who was mourning the love of his life."

"Did your dad know she had a heart condition? Or did it happen suddenly?"

"It was sudden. Unexpected." She paused, took a breath, remembered the jasmine fragrance her mother used to wear. "We buried her in a white casket, in a white dress."

He brushed her hand. "We should put pictures up of our parents. Old photos. Old memories. Family is important."

"I wish it didn't matter."

"Because of why I married you?"

"Yes." She turned away to view the city, to see other rooftops, other downtown buildings.

"You married me for the same reason," he said.

"I know." She shifted her gaze, looking at him once again, thinking about how much it hurt to love him, to be drowning in it. "But we should have married for love. The way our parents did," she added, bringing up both couples.

Aaron didn't respond. He didn't say a word. But he reached out and held her.

Making her hurt even more.

Eleven

When Talia stepped back, Aaron didn't want to let her go. But she refused his affection.

"What's wrong?" he asked.

"Nothing," she responded.

"Come on. What's going on?"

"I don't want to talk about it." A small breeze blew, making beautiful havoc of her hair.

When she turned away, he touched her shoulder and felt her tense. "Don't shut me out."

"Why? Why does it matter?" She rounded on him, her eyes, those stunning blue eyes, gutted with pain.

Suddenly Aaron knew. "It happened, didn't it, Tai? You fell in love with me?"

"Yes. On our wedding night." The words came out broken. "But I'd been fighting it all along."

He wanted to gloat, to say I told you so, but her admission overwhelmed him.

Because the past came rushing back. Not the bad memories, but the good ones, the images only lovers could share.

"I understand," he told her, reaching out to touch her again.

"How can you?" she snapped, pushing him away. "How can you know what I'm going through?" She walked over to the fence rail, to the steel bars that guarded the rooftop ledge. "You shouldn't have proposed to me the way you did."

Guilt gripped him hard and fast, squeezing him like a noose. But he defended his actions. "You're the one who put the revenge idea in my head. You brought it up first. Sleep with me for revenge for all that."

"That's not the same as marrying someone. I should have known better."

His pulse hammered a hard-hitting rhythm. She made him ache, deep inside, like she used to. "Don't say that. Don't talk as if we shouldn't be together."

"Why does it matter if we're together? If both of us don't love each other, then what's the point?"

He fought the air in his lungs, trying to release it, trying to breathe. "Give me a chance, Tai."

"How? Why?"

He didn't respond, and silence shifted between them, like shadows, like the memories berating his mind: the day they'd met, the first time they'd kissed, smiled, laughed, had sweet, syrupy sex. He remembered every man-on-fire detail, every call-her-at-midnight, he-missed-hearing-her-voice moment.

"Because I think it's happening to me, too," he finally said. Now, he thought. Right now. Like a lifeline to the past, a vein that wasn't supposed to bleed.

"That isn't funny, Aaron."

"Do I look like I'm being funny?" He was teetering on the edge of fear, on the brink of destruction.

She searched his gaze. "So Carrie was right? You've been fighting your feelings, too?"

He nodded, felt his chest constrict, hated himself for it. "If you left me, I'd die."

Her voice turned shaky. "I didn't say I was leaving."

"Not in so many words, but…" He tightened his fingers, locking and unlocking them. "If this doesn't work, you'll walk out on me. And I'll be living in déjà vu land, annihilated by the woman I love." He cursed, battled the lingering fear, the last-ditch effort to come clean. "The woman I've probably always loved."

She swayed on her feet. "Do you know what it feels like to hear you say that?"

"The same way it felt to hear you say it," he told her, knowing they'd come too far to turn back. They'd just gotten their hearts involved. Fully. Completely. Like before.

Only this time, they were married.

She looked up him, all soft and sensitive, all blond and vulnerable. "Does this change the rules?"

"Does it change them for you?" he asked.

She nodded, her voice still a little shaky. "We should be compromising. It's what we should have done from the beginning."

"Then you'll give in, Talia? You'll learn about my heritage?"

"If I do, what's your compromise? What will you do to make our relationship work?"

He moved closer, wished his pulse wasn't speeding out of control. "I'll be the best husband I can be."

"What about your family?"

"They'll accept you, Talia. Once they see how hard you're trying."

"What if they don't? Would you defend me? Would you stand by my side?"

He didn't want to consider the possibility, to imagine his family leaving him in a lurch.

She pressed him for an answer, making him face her question. "Would you?"

He released the breath he'd been fighting earlier, letting the pent-up air out of his lungs. "Yes." What choice would he have? He couldn't make Talia suffer any more than he already had. "But this has to be more than lip service. You have to make an honest effort, to care about being part of my culture."

"I do," she told him, "or I did all those years ago when you denied me the opportunity to."

"Then everything will be fine." He took her in his

arms, reliving the raw, ragged, desperation of being in love. "We'll make it work."

"I hope so." She put her head on his shoulder. "God, I hope so."

The loft buzzed with activity. Talia had eaten dinner with her dad, her brothers, her new stepson and her husband, and now they shared the living room, enjoying each other's company.

Ron Gibson, Talia's father, sent her a daddy's-girl wink, and she smiled. He was a big man, over six feet, with broad shoulders and light brown hair that was turning gray. He'd always made her feel safe, even if she rarely confided in him. Just knowing that he cared was enough. But it was Aaron who'd made a difference.

She glanced at her husband, still reeling from the promise they'd made, from the compromise they'd agreed upon. Would it work? Could it be this easy?

Aaron sat next to his son on the floor in front of the coffee table, helping the boy draw a picture with the art set Talia had given him for his birthday. Her brothers were involved too, giving Danny instructions. The picture was a portrait of all of them—Talia and the men in her life.

"Give me more muscles," Brad, her oldest brother said about his crayon image.

"And a higher forehead," Casey, the youngest Gibson male put in, teasing Brad about his receding hairline. Casey wore his blond locks in a windblown, street-tough, motorcycle-mechanic mess.

Keith, the middle son, another grease monkey with a head full of hair, chuckled at the running joke.

Talia rolled her eyes. Sometimes her brothers seemed like overgrown kids, even though they were men in their late thirties and early forties. Still, she loved being their baby sister.

Danny looked up. He'd added two bicep bumps onto Brad's body, giving him the requested muscles. He seemed a bit perplexed about the higher forehead.

Talia moved closer to him. "You're doing a great job. It's a good drawing."

"Thank you." He smiled at her. "I tried to make you pretty."

"And you did." With red lips, she noticed, and black shoes that were supposed to be high heels.

"Daddy said I could help you learn to talk Luiseño."

"I know. I'm really looking forward to it." She and Aaron had agreed that Danny should be an integral part of her studies.

"Danny goes to the Pechanga School," Aaron said to Talia's father and brothers. "The students are educated bilingually in English and Luiseño. For now, the school goes from preschool to first grade. But the tribe hopes to expand to higher grades in the future."

"Hey, that's cool. Will you help us talk Luiseño, too?" Casey asked Danny. "Me, Keith, Brad and our dad?"

The boy gave a vigorous nod. He seemed intrigued by his new family, particularly his outspoken Uncle Casey. Not that he hadn't been paying close attention to Talia. She sensed that Danny thought she was pretty, like the lady in his drawing.

"I'm in kindergarten," Danny said. "Our teacher told us about the Pechanga Tribal Sea, and we got to put Native plants in a garden. I could show everyone how to do that, too."

Talia looked at Aaron and smiled. He and Jeannie had raised a good-hearted, well-mannered child.

"I don't know how to talk Apache or do much Apache stuff," the boy admitted.

Suddenly Aaron frowned. "We'll have to work on that." He addressed Talia's family. "Danny is being raised with the Luiseño, with his grandmother's people. He hasn't had much exposure to his Apache side."

Talia's father sat back in his chair. "My kids have Swedish ancestry, but they were never taught anything about it."

"Was your wife Swedish?" Aaron asked.

"Yes, she was."

"She was beautiful," Aaron told him. "Talia showed me her picture."

"My daughter looks like her."

"She certainly does."

Aaron reached for her hand, and she felt wonderfully warm inside. Being in love with her husband and knowing that he loved her made their vows seem real. Honest, she thought. The kind of marriage she'd dreamed about in the past.

He turned to kiss her, giving her a nuzzling peck on the cheek.

When things turned quiet, Casey interrupted. "Where's that dessert you promised, sis?"

Talia tried to not get flustered, to not feel foolish about an innocent moment of intimacy. "Ice-cream sundaes? We have to make them."

Danny popped up. "All of us?"

"Yep. All of us." She stood, too.

"Then, let's go." Casey reached for Danny and heaved the boy into his arms. "Let's put extra whipped cream and junk on ours."

Talia had purchased every sweet, syrupy, gooey sundae fixing known to man, giving Danny and Casey the opportunity to make an ice-cream coated mess.

"He's good with kids," Aaron whispered about Casey. "He should have some of his own."

"He'd planned to, but he got caught up in irreconcilable differences," she whispered back, wishing all of her brothers weren't divorced. That her family history didn't include so many failed marriages.

At ten o'clock, Aaron and Talia tucked Danny in. They sat on the edge of his bed, and he looked at them through heavy eyelids.

Aaron skimmed his hand along his son's forehead, moving his bangs out of his eyes. "Good night, buddy."

"Do I have to go sleep, Daddy?"

He'd already read Danny a story and said a prayer with him. "It's way past your bedtime."

"But I like staying up."

"I know, but it's late, and everyone went home."

"You and Talia are still here."

"We're going to bed soon, too."

"That's not fair." Danny looked snug as a pitch-a-fit bug with his race car-printed quilt and toys-galore room. He grabbed the stuffed lion next to him and tugged it closer, making the kind of face kids make when they don't get their way. "I want to stay up."

Talia came to the rescue. "How about this? If we all go to bed now and get enough sleep, we can get up early and you can help me fix breakfast. We can make pancakes and put lots of syrup on them."

"Okay." The boy smiled at her. "Then I can teach you to talk Luiseño."

"You've got a deal." She leaned over to kiss him, to brush her lips across his cheek. She kissed the lion, too, giving the king of the jungle equal attention.

Aaron couldn't think of a more poignant moment: his new wife, his child and the tenderness developing between them.

Talk about admitting the truth, Aaron thought. About acknowledging his feelings. He wanted the perfect marriage. He wanted love and commitment and everything that went with it.

When Danny closed his eyes, and Aaron and Talia said a final good night to him, they left on a night-light, creating a soft glow.

From there they headed to the master suite and got ready for bed, locking the door behind them.

Aaron watched Talia put on a pair of silk pajamas.

"You're wasting your time," he said.

"On what?"

"Those." He opened the top button on her pretty PJs. "I'm going to take them off you."

"Are you?" She slipped her arms around his neck and kissed him, making him want her even more.

"Yes, ma'am, I am." He inhaled the fragrance she wore, the perfume called Trouble. "I want to make a baby with you."

She blinked, stepped back, threw him off-kilter. "Now? Tonight?"

"Seeing you with Danny makes me want to have another one."

"So quickly?"

He frowned at her. "This isn't the first time we've talked about this."

She frowned, too. "I never agreed to get pregnant right away."

"That was before." He glanced at the feminine touches she'd added to his room, the gypsy-like shawls draped over lampshades, the scented candles, the engraved jewelry box. "Now that you love me, that we're compromising on our future, what's stopping you?"

"Your motivation," she told him.

"Meaning what? That I'm trying to get you pregnant so my family will accept you more easily?"

"Aren't you?"

"No." Feeling like a disgruntled caveman, he imagined carrying her off to bed and having his mate-with-me way with her. "But it wouldn't hurt."

"That's my point," she said. "I don't want to win

your family over because I'm carrying your child. I want them to like me for who I am."

Aaron conceded. He wanted that, too. He wanted his mother and his aunt to respect her, to appreciate her effort. "It's okay, Tai. We can wait to have babies."

She climbed into bed. "Do you still want to be with me tonight?"

He smiled, moved closer, reached for her. "Is that a rhetorical question?"

Twelve

With dawn filtering through the blinds, Talia awakened next to her husband. The covers were bunched around his hips and his hair fell in morning-after disarray. She imagined that she looked warm and well loved, too.

Mesmerized, she touched his jaw, skimming her finger along the hardened edge. He stirred, mumbling a few incoherent words. She waited, but he didn't open his eyes, so she let him sleep.

Talia climbed out of bed and smoothed her silk ensemble. After making love last night, she and Aaron had put their pajamas back on and unlocked their door, giving Danny access to their room.

And with good reason.

A second later, the door creaked open and Talia saw Danny through the opening. His hair, spiked with a boyhood surge of static electricity, stuck out at odd angles.

Feeling like a new mom, she smiled and crooked her finger, inviting him inside. Suddenly he bounded into the room, gave her a knee-jarring bear hug and jumped onto the bed, waking up his dad with the ex-hilaration of a rambunctious puppy.

Talia's head whirred like a press-and-spin top. Her experience with children was limited. But Aaron's wasn't. As tired as he was, he grabbed Danny and wrestled with him, playing the way males often do.

The five-year-old squealed with Daddy-loves-me glee and initiated a pillow fight.

Unsure of what else to do, Talia slipped into the bathroom to wash her face, comb her hair and brush her teeth. When she returned, the bed looked like a war zone.

But both boys were grinning.

"Can we make breakfast now?" Danny asked Talia.

"Absolutely." She glanced at Aaron. "Are you going to cook with us?"

He shook his head, smoothed his messy hair and gave her a happily married smile. "I'm going to take a shower. You can call me when it's ready."

"We will." This came from Danny, who skidded across the floor toward Talia and grabbed her hand.

After that, they were off, zooming down the hall.

Danny didn't waste any time. He took a chair from the dining room and slid it into the kitchen, placing it at the counter so he could reach everything.

"Now you're taller than me," Talia said.

"'Cause you're not wearing your big shoes." He wiggled like a happy-go-lucky worm. "Can we make those little pancakes?"

"The silver dollar kind?"

He nodded. "Daddy orders those when we go out to breakfast."

She removed a box of instant pancake mix. "And what do you order?"

"A kid's meal." He made a serious expression. "'Cause I'm a kid."

A sweet, overly helpful kid. Before she could stop him, he ripped into the package, making a mess. But what the hey. This was her introduction to parenthood.

Talia offered him a big plastic bowl and showed him how to measure the mix and add water to it. He made an even bigger mess when he tried to stir it.

The powder flew out of the bowl, dusting the counters. Danny's pajamas took a dusty coating, too. And so did Talia's.

Finally, she helped him create the right consistency. He wanted to push his chair in front of the stove so he could cook the pancakes, but she wouldn't let him. New parent or not, the stove was off-limits.

She put him to work, folding a slew of napkins

into what were supposed to be bird-like shapes. While he kept busy, she scrambled eggs, fried ham and flipped the silver dollar flapjacks.

"Wanna talk Luiseño now?" he asked.

"Sure. But first, what does Luiseño mean?"

"It came from a mission. There are six bands of Luiseños. Me and Mommy and Daddy are from the Pechanga Band."

"And what does that mean?" she asked, willing to be tutored by a child, by a boy who understood his culture, who learned about it everyday in school.

"It means place where the water drips." He paused to fold another napkin. "That's 'cause it's the name of a spring at the mountain where the people from a long time ago lived after they had to move."

She suspected that he was referring to a forced eviction, a common occurrence in Native history. "So you became known as the Pechanga, the people who live at the spring at the mountain?"

"Uh-huh. If you're gonna talk Luiseño, then you gotta sing Luiseño songs, too."

She agreed, and he proceeded to teach her a story-telling song, something he'd learned in school. She knew she wasn't getting it, at least not very well, but he promised to keep helping her. She wondered if he would grow up to be a teacher.

When the food was ready, the lesson ended, the unfamiliar words still buzzing in her head.

"Go get your daddy," she told Danny. "And I'll set the table."

"Okay." He flew off like one of his paper birds and returned with Aaron in tow.

Her husband entered the kitchen in jeans and a T-shirt, with his damp hair combed straight back, exposing the angles of his face. Talia wasn't sure how to greet him, so she offered him a good morning peck, grazing his freshly shaven skin.

He rolled his eyes and swung her into his arms, bending her backward for a dramatic, tango-like kiss. Danny laughed at his father's antics and Talia pretended to swoon, fanning herself with her hand.

When he released her, her heart pounded for real. So much for pretending.

"I love you," she said.

"I love you, too," he responded, holding her against his heart, with his son, the little boy who was fast becoming her own, by their side.

After work on Tuesday, Talia shopped with Carrie at a trend-setting bridal shop located at the edge of Beverly Hills and Hollywood.

Carrie was helping Talia find a matron-of-honor dress, something that would fit the wedding she and Thunder had planned.

"We talked about get married right on the beach," Carrie said. "But then we found this amazing little hilltop chapel that overlooks the water, so that's what we're going to do. This way it can be formal. We still have another two months to plan it. We set a late-spring date."

"It sounds beautiful. Perfect for a California wedding."

Carrie stopped at the entrance of the store. "Are you disappointed that you got married in Vegas? That you did it so quickly?"

"No. I'm okay with how things happened now that Aaron loves me."

The other woman gave her a sly grin. "I told you he was fighting it."

"And you were right." They went inside and glanced around. "What color should I be looking for?"

"Lavender or pale blue." Carrie paused. "I chose colors that complement the ocean. I'll be carrying a crystal and seashell bouquet with silver ribbon. Your bouquet and the men's boutonnieres will be designed the same way, but without the shells."

"What's your dress like?" Talia asked, caught up in the splendor.

"It's a sleeveless gown with a crystal-beaded bodice." Carrie touched her tummy. "It has an Empire waist, so there's plenty of room for the baby. Thunder was with me when I ordered it."

"Is it strange marrying the same man twice?"

The other woman smiled. "Wonderfully strange. Our parents are ecstatic."

"My father is happy, too. But Aaron's mother and his aunt…" Talia frowned. "Aaron is convinced they'll accept me. But I'm not so sure."

"You're doing everything you can to win them over." Carrie walked over to a rack filled with designer dresses. "Aaron told Thunder that you're learning the Luiseño language. How can Aaron's mother not appreciate that?"

"I only learned one Luiseño song. And I can't sing it very well."

"But you're trying. That's what matters." Carrie turned, looked at her. "By the way, I promised Thunder that I would warn you about our engagement party."

"Warn me?"

"We're having a get-together at our house, and the invitations are going out today. Thunder is sending one to Aaron's family. He thinks it's the right thing to do."

Talia told herself not to react, not to worry about seeing Aaron's family. But her nerves betrayed her. "That's understandable. Thunder is related to them, too. Does Aaron know?"

"Thunder intends to tell him. With everything that's been going on, he wanted both of you to know ahead of time. But something like this was bound to happen sooner or later. Maybe it'll be good to get it over with."

"And maybe Aaron's family won't go to the party."

"It's hard to say. But either way, Thunder thought it would be rude not to invite them. They're looking forward to our wedding, so how could we not tell them about the engagement party?"

"You couldn't. You shouldn't." Before things got tense and Talia spoiled the shopping, she focused on the task at hand, needing to change the subject, needing to clear her mind. "Speaking of your wedding…I still have to find a dress."

Carrie angled her head, smiled a little. "Maybe you should wear blue. You look amazing in blue."

"Thank you." Aaron liked her in blue, too. Because of her eyes, she thought. With a deep breath, Talia browsed the rack, then chose a sleeveless gown with a scarf hem. "How about this? And this?" She reached for a classic A-line silk, a dress that worked well for any formal occasion.

"They're both beautiful. You should try them on. What do you think of this one?" Carrie lifted another dress. "I like the embroidery, and the way it cascades in the back." Suddenly another gown caught her eye. "Oh, my. This is even better."

Talia studied the vintage, glamour-girl fashion. "That would be gorgeous with a pair of gauntlet gloves."

"And a crystal bouquet."

Excited by her prospects, Talia headed for the dressing room, a salesclerk fast on her heels, eager to help with all of the buttons and zippers.

When she emerged wearing the vintage-style gown, Carrie caught her breath. "I think that's perfect on you. Do you like it?"

"Yes. Very much." It reminded her of something her mother would have worn, and that made her feel special. She turned from side to side, checking out her reflection. "Should I shop for gloves to go with it?"

"Absolutely." Carrie sent her an excited-bride smile. "Do you see what that dress does to your eyes?"

Talia smiled, too. She suspected Aaron was going to love it. "Are the men wearing tuxedos?"

"Yes. Our handsome men. How lucky are we?"

"Very lucky." Only Talia hadn't forgotten about her in-laws and the upcoming party she'd been warned about. Somehow that didn't make her feel particularly lucky.

After she and Carrie parted ways and she returned to the loft, she found Aaron on the rooftop patio, gazing at the evening sky.

He turned to look at her, to hold out his hand, encouraging her to join him. She sat next to him at the table and noticed that he was drinking an espresso from the coffee bar across the street.

"Did you find a dress?" he asked.

She nodded. "Yes, but it isn't ready yet. It needs to be altered. It's too long, even with my heels." She decided to move the conversation along. "Did Thunder tell you about the party?"

"That he invited my family? Yes, he did." Aaron frowned. "I called my mom and aunt about it."

"You did?" Talia's pulse nearly beat its way out of her body. "Are they going to attend?"

He nodded. "They're both coming."

"Did you tell them about our compromise?"

"Yes. I told them how much I love you. And that you love me, too. I explained that our marriage wasn't about revenge anymore."

"And they're okay with everything now?"

"I think they're still trying to process it."

Her heart sank. "So they're still upset about me being your wife?"

"It isn't as bad as it sounds. They promised to give you a chance, to talk to you at the party, to get to know you."

She watched steam rise from his cup, then dissipate into the air. "Did you tell them that Danny was teaching me their language?"

"Yes, but they didn't say much about that."

Her heart sank even lower. "Because I'll always be white. Because I'll always be the non-Native girl you married."

"They're not bigots, Tai. They don't have a problem with Thunder's wife. Or Jeannie's new husband."

"Yes, but they've always had a problem with me. If they didn't, you would have married me instead of Jeannie."

"I didn't marry you because of the vow I made to my father," he explained. "Because of how important it was to my family." He made a tight expression. "At the time, I was determined to live by it, to respect my family's wishes. And now I'm asking them to respect mine, to accept you, to appreciate your interest in their culture."

"And use this party as a catalyst to help bridge the gap?" Talia tried to relax. "As long as I can count on you. As long as you're beside me."

"I will be," he responded. "Every step of the way."

* * *

On the day of the party, Aaron stepped out of the shower, dried off and put on his robe. He went into the bedroom to check on Talia and saw her sitting at her antique vanity, fixing her hair.

He stood behind her, watching the way she moved, the way the big gold barrette in her hand caught the light. She met his gaze in the mirror and they looked at each other. Deeply, he thought. At that unspoken moment, they were the only two people on earth.

"I'm nervous," she said, shattering the silence.

"Everything will be okay," he replied.

She fastened the barrette, creating a ladylike ponytail at the nape of her neck.

He tried not to frown, to admit that he was nervous, too. What if he was wrong about his mother and his aunt? What if they turned their noses up at Talia tonight?

No, he thought. They wouldn't do that. They'd promised to give her a chance.

"How can you be sure?" she asked. "How can you be sure that everything will be okay?"

He thought about his childhood, about the prayers, the songs, the right-from-wrong stories. He'd been weaned on tradition, on honorable values. "I just do."

Because if his family disrespected his wife, the woman learning their language and embracing their culture, then everything they claimed to represent would be a lie. And for Aaron that was inconceivable. He needed to believe that his heritage, the part of him he'd fought so hard to preserve, would never be in vain.

Talia changed the subject, throwing him off kilter. "Do these boots look all right?"

He squinted. "What?"

"These boots." She stood up and showed him her outfit: a tan skirt, a matching top and brown leather boots with a barely-there heel.

"Sure. I think they're fine."

"I don't look too short?"

He came toward her, reached out and drew her into his arms, hitching his chin to the top of her head. "I like how small you are."

She glanced up at him. "I'd prefer to wear something with a higher heel, but I'm trying to present a more conservative image, so I bought these for tonight."

"To impress my mom and my aunt?" Suddenly the thought troubled him. Initially he'd wanted Talia to do whatever she could to prove herself, but seeing her like this, watching her alter her appearance didn't seem right. He was preserving his identity, holding onto who he was, and she was struggling to become someone new. "Shoes don't make the man. Or woman, in this case."

"What does that mean? What are you trying to say?"

"Wear heels. The higher the better."

She blinked at him. "Are you trying to sabotage this for me?"

"No. I'm trying to let you be who you are." He

removed the barrette from her hair and ran his hands through the pale blond strands.

She gave him a bewildered look. "You're confusing me."

"I don't want you going overboard. Taking a genuine interest in my culture is enough. You don't have to talk and walk and dress different. That's not what this is about."

"So I can wear red lipstick? Put on a fancy belt? More jewelry?"

"I'd be disappointed if you didn't. I'm attracted to that side of you, Tai. I'm in love with the femme fatale I married."

She kissed him, deep and slow, giving him a sexual charge with her body, all those luscious curves, pressed against him.

"Be careful," he told her, as she caught the edge of his robe. "I'm naked underneath."

"I can tell." She bumped the hardness. "I'm going to seduce you when we get back."

He gulped air into his lungs. "Promise?"

"Absolutely. I'm making love to my husband tonight."

"Then let's get this party over with," he teased, determined to support his wife, to encourage her to keep to her identity.

And charm his family just the same.

Thirteen

Talia and Aaron didn't arrive early, but they weren't fashionably late either. Aaron drove around, searching for a parking spot on a typically crowded side street, and Talia glanced out the windshield. She could see the ocean in the distance.

"Maybe we should look for a house near here," she said. They'd been too busy with their work schedules to start house hunting, but they'd been meaning to contact a Realtor.

He found a parking spot and wedged his shiny silver sports car into it. "That's fine with me. I like the beach." He smiled, caught her eye. "I could get a boat and name it after you."

She smiled, too. "A speed boat."

"Right." He leaned over to kiss her cheek. "Something that moves dangerously fast."

They got out of the car and took to the sidewalk, where her man-killer shoes with their stiletto heels drilled into the night.

Thunder and Carrie's house was two blocks away, closer to the beach, closer to the moonlit ocean. Talia reached for Aaron's hand and forced herself to breathe. She was afraid she might hyperventilate.

"Relax," he told her. "It's just a party."

"Right." With his mom and his aunt sitting in judgment. "Maybe I should have worn the flat boots."

"Don't start, Tai. You look gorgeous."

And flashy, she thought, with her tousled hair, bold jewelry, smoky eyeliner and racy-red lipstick. "Are you sure I didn't overdo it?"

"You get fixed up like that every day."

"Maybe I overdo it at work, too."

"Not a chance." He stopped walking, shifted to look at her. "You were born to turn heads, to get noticed."

"Like my mom?" She relaxed a little. "My dad used to say that beauty was in her blood."

"It's in yours, too." He squeezed her hand and they resumed walking, reaching Thunder and Carrie's house within minutes.

The tri-level structure faced the sea, and the sidewalk in front of it led to eclectic shops and trendy eateries.

Carrie greeted them at the door, glowing like the expectant mother she was. "My two favorite people," she said, inviting them inside.

Talia gave the other woman a hug. The house was filled with friends and family, eating, drinking and talking. Classic rock played in the background, adding a thumping rhythm.

"Where's my cousin?" Aaron asked.

"I'm right here." Thunder came around the corner and handed Aaron a beer and Talia a glass of champagne. "I'm glad to see you guys."

"And we're glad to be here." Aaron toasted the engaged couple.

"Roberta and Lynn aren't here yet," Thunder said, referring to Aaron's mother and aunt. "But they will be." He waited a beat. "You understand why I invited them, don't you?"

Aaron responded, "Of course I do. All of our family is here. It's only right. Don't worry about it, Thunder. Everything is going to be fine."

Talia forced a smile, trying to get into the party mode. "Yes, it is." She paused, gestured to the buffet table. "Everything looks so good. I'm anxious to try the appetizers."

Fifteen minutes later, Roberta and Lynn still hadn't arrived. But Talia didn't mind. If anything, it gave her time to relax. By then, she'd picked at the food, snacking on shrimp puffs and crab and cucumber rolls.

Finally she and Aaron mingled, separating to talk to different people. He offered to stay beside her the entire time, but she told him that once his family showed up, they could reunite. So for now, he joined a group of men on the balcony, and she socialized with some employees from SPEC. Then she spotted Dylan from across the room. He noticed her, too. They met halfway, smiling at each other.

"You're as hot as ever," he said.

"And you're the ultimate flirt." She saw a few single girls checking him out. "The Trueno baby."

He raised his eyebrows at that. "Thunder's kid is going to be the Trueno baby. I'm the younger brother."

"So you are." She and Aaron had been keeping in touch with Dylan by phone, keeping abreast of Julia. Not that there had been anything pertinent to discuss. Dylan was still searching for her.

"Is Aaron a good husband?" he asked. "Or does he suck?"

She laughed a little. "He's amazing. The best."

"Really?" Another eyebrow raise. Then a slightly crooked grin. "I guess that means I don't stand a chance of stealing you away from him?"

"I'm afraid not." Their gazes locked, and he turned serious. She could see the shift of emotion in his eyes. He was teasing her, playing the bad boy bachelor, but Julia was there, in the back of his mind. "You'll find her, Dylan."

"Or grow old trying."

When they both fell silent, he excused himself to get a beer. She let him go, watching the single girls check him out again. She wondered if he would go home with one of them tonight or if he would head back to Nevada, back to the missing woman occupying his mind.

Talia decided to get some air, to take a moment to watch the sea. Still nursing the same glass of champagne, she went outside and stood on the sidewalk in front of the house, where the sand was only inches away. An aggressive breeze caught her hair, blowing it around her face.

She sipped from the crystal flute, thinking about how breathtaking the scenery was, how strong, how passionate.

Then footsteps sounded. She turned, froze like a statue and felt her heart vault to her throat.

Roberta and Lynn had arrived. They stopped walking, and the three of them gazed uncomfortably at each other. Lynn, Aaron's aunt, gave her a blatantly disapproving look, checking out her ensemble. Roberta, Aaron's mother, kept her expression a bit more subdued.

Talia clutched her glass. Should she say hello? Or just let them pass?

"You shouldn't have married him," Lynn said suddenly.

For a moment Talia wasn't sure what to do, how to respond. She hadn't envisioned getting trapped like this. She looked around for her husband, but she didn't see him.

"I love Aaron," she finally said, moving toward the porch and setting her drink on the bottom step.

Lynn merely snorted. "You're going to ruin his life. Just like before."

Talia tempered her emotions, trying to be diplomatic, trying to maintain her composure. "Aaron and I hurt each other. But that was years ago. Things are different now." She turned to Roberta. "Do you believe that I love your son?"

Aaron's mother didn't respond. But Lynn did. She crossed her arms, where her shawl bunched into a mass of crocheted fringe. Her hair was blowing in the breeze, too. "I don't believe it. What kind of woman marries a man to get back at his family?"

"I'm sorry for that," Talia said. "Terribly sorry. At the time I accepted his proposal I was still struggling with the past."

"You want to talk about the past?" Lynn batted her hair away from her face. "About how you destroyed his first marriage?"

Just then, a masculine voice caught their attention. Aaron was standing in the open doorway. "I can't believe this is happening. That you're doing this to Talia. To me." He came outside, rounding on his aunt, on his mother. "I trusted you. I trusted both of you."

Lynn tried to state her case. "She isn't right for you. She isn't—"

He cut her off. "Someone my family would have chosen? I've lived my entire life trying to honor our traditions, to do what was expected of me. I've been the loyal son, the respectful nephew. But I'm done.

I've had it." He narrowed his gaze, hurt and anger flashing in his eyes. "Talia took an interest in our culture because of me. Because I thought it mattered. But now I know that it doesn't." He looked straight at his aunt. "You promised that you would give her a chance, but instead you're being rude to her, making me ashamed. And you…" He turned to his mother, his voice hard, chipped. "You're being a coward. Letting Aunt Lynn speak for you."

Roberta's eyes got watery, but she didn't come to her own defense. When Aaron reached for Talia's hand and led her away from the party, insisting it was time to go home, his mother just stood there.

Talia glanced back, silently imploring Roberta to stop them. But she didn't.

The loft seemed vacant, as hollow as Aaron's emotions. When Talia walked across the floor, her shoes made a rat-a-tat-tat, a semi-automatic sound.

"We shouldn't have left," she said.

Aaron frowned at her. "Whose side are you on?"

"Yours. But I don't think we gave your mother a chance."

Refusing to listen, he went into the bedroom to remove his jacket, to toss it over a chair. His shoes came next. He literally kicked them into a corner.

Talia followed him. "Don't shut me out. Don't let this ruin what we have."

He sat on the edge of the bed and looked at his

wife. She stood near the mirrored vanity, where the glass reflected bottles, lotions and scattered cosmetics. "Then don't feel badly for my mom."

"I can't help it. She looked so sad."

Talia went over the dresser and lit a small grouping of candles, and Aaron wondered if she was trying to purify the air, to cleanse the negative energy.

"I don't think your mother meant for things to turn out this way," she said, lighting the final candle.

He watched the wick ignite. "Then why didn't she say something? Why didn't she speak up?" He tugged his hand through his hair, pushing the beach-blown strands away from his forehead. He could still see the ocean in his mind, still feel the ravage of the wind. "She disrespected us, Tai. And my aunt…" He didn't even want to say her name, to acknowledge that she'd helped raise him.

Talia sat next to him. "I'm sorry things turned out this way."

"You warned me from the beginning. You knew my family wouldn't come through." He put his hand on her knee. "I should have listened to you."

"I think your mom wanted to come through."

"Stop saying that." He curled his fingers around the fabric of her skirt. "I'm done with my family, with my heritage, with all the lies they taught me."

"You're choosing me over them? Over your culture?" Her expression fell. "That's what I wanted in the beginning. But I don't want that now. Please, don't make a hasty decision. Don't act on impulse.

Give your mom a little more time." She paused, covered his hand with hers. "And your aunt, too."

"I can't." His childhood seemed like a hodge-podge of shattered memories. "I don't feel like the same person any more."

"But you are." She squeezed his fingers. "You're still the man I married, the man I fell in love with." She caught his gaze. "And you'll always be the boy who made a promise to his dad."

"How can you say that? What my father asked of me was wrong. He should have encouraged me to marry a woman I loved, no matter who she was."

"Your mother changed his life, so he thought a Pechanga woman would change yours, too. And in some ways, Jeannie did. If you hadn't married her, you wouldn't have had Danny."

He gazed into her eyes, touched by her words, but confused by them, too. "How can you be so gracious about all of this?"

"Because I love you. And I love your son."

He moved closer to her, appreciating her sincerity. "It still hurts, Tai. What my mother and my aunt did still hurts."

"I know." She lifted her face, her mouth only inches from his. "It hurt me, too. I wanted them to trust me. To believe that I was being sincere."

"And they should have. I already told them how much you love me. How much I love you." Aaron took a rough breath. Suddenly he wanted Talia to kiss him, to take the edge off their emotions, to help them forget that their hearts had been damaged.

When silence lapsed between them, neither of them moved. They just keep looking at each other, with colored wax melting, with flames on candles flourishing.

"Are you going to seduce me?" he asked, breaking the silence. "Are you going to keep the promise you made earlier?"

Her voice was soft and low. "Is that what you want me to do?"

"Yes." He waited; he watched, needing her more than he'd ever needed her before.

Taking control, she reached for the buttons on his shirt, undoing them one by one. When she went after the zipper on his trousers, he nuzzled her neck, inhaling her scent.

She nudged him down, climbing on top of him, making his pulse pound between his legs. By now he was half-naked and desperate for her.

But she made him wait. She kissed him sweet and slow, letting the tension build even more. He put his hands all over her, tugging at her clothes.

"Is this what you want?" She removed her blouse and exposed her bra.

"That and more." He unhooked the pretty lace barrier and let it slide down her shoulders. Then he licked her nipples, one right after the other, making them peak.

She ran her fingers through his hair and made a

breathy sound. He used his teeth, just a little, just enough to make her shiver, to create goose bumps on her skin.

They rolled over the bed and kissed once again, mouth-to-mouth, tongue-to-tongue. When she removed her panties, he smiled. She was still wearing her skirt and the high-heeled shoes that made bullet-like sounds.

"Are we going to do it like this?" he asked, referring to their partially clothed state.

"Yes, we are." She adjusted his trousers to accommodate her, pushing his boxers down with them. A condom came next, with Talia making good use of it.

Aaron lifted his hips, giving her free reign. When she bunched her skirt and straddled him, he gripped her waist, anxious to join with her.

They made love in a tangle of bedding and rumpled clothes, kissing and touching.

Clawing their way into each other's souls.

Fourteen

Aaron walked into the living room and closed his cell phone. "Thunder and Carrie are coming over around noon, so I told them they could stay for lunch. Is that okay?"

Talia looked up from the book she was reading. She and Aaron were spending a lazy day at home, pretending that they could cope with the turmoil in their lives. "Of course it is."

"They want to talk to us about last night. About the party." He frowned and sat in the chair across from her.

"Can you blame them?" She dog-eared the novel and placed it on the coffee table. "We left without saying anything, without telling them what happened."

"I'm sure my aunt gave them an earful." He frowned again. "Blaming all of this on us."

Talia studied her husband. The midmorning sun filtered through the skylight, sending a soft-hued sheen through his hair. But it didn't take the edge off his features. "I know it hurts, Aaron, but we should try to make amends with your mom. And your aunt," she added, knowing that would be an even bigger challenge. But to her, it was worth the risk. In a roundabout way, she'd won the revenge game. She'd triumphed over his family, and it made her feel sick inside.

He set his jaw. "No way. They had their chance. Just let it go, Tai."

She looked directly at him. "What point is there in being bitter? In not trying to salvage what you had with them?"

"I asked you to let it go." He returned her straightforward gaze. "Promise me that you won't show up on their doorstep. That you won't try to fix this on your own."

"I just want everything to be all right."

"It is all right. I have you. And Danny. We're a family now."

"But it isn't supposed to be us against your other family." She took a ragged breath, thinking about Danny, about his innocence. "What are you going to say to your son? That you don't love his grandma or his great-aunt anymore?"

"I never said I didn't love them any more." He moved back and forth along the floor.

"Then try to make peace with them."

"How? By forcing them to accept you? I already tried that." He stopped pacing. "Promise me, Tai. Promise you'll let it go."

She glanced at her bracelet, at the birthstones she and Aaron shared with his parents. Aaron had wanted her to feel closer to his parents, to have a connection to them. But that was lost now. "Maybe you're right. Maybe it's wishful thinking." Maybe the tears she'd seen in his mother's eyes weren't enough.

Preparing for Thunder and Carrie, Talia made lunch, keeping herself busy, her mind running rampant.

What if Roberta's tears continued? What if she cried forever? Mourning the son who'd shunned her?

Then again, it was Roberta's fault that Aaron felt the way he did. He'd given his mother the opportunity to be kind to Talia, to respect their marriage.

By the time Thunder and Carrie arrived, the food was ready. Everyone ate the spinach salad and the chicken and dumplings, but only Carrie had dessert, indulging in chocolate chip cookies.

"I shouldn't have invited your mom and your aunt to the party," Thunder said to Aaron. "I should have known better."

"You were just trying to be fair," Aaron responded. "To include everyone. This isn't your fault."

Talia and Carrie didn't voice their opinions. They listened to their husbands discuss the situation, with Thunder supporting Aaron. If his family had disrespected his wife, he would have walked away, too.

Finally the couples separated. The men went to the patio roof to have a beer, and the women cleaned up the kitchen.

Carrie transferred the salad bowls to the sink. "You're having second thoughts, aren't you?"

"Yes, but Aaron asked me to let it go."

Carrie turned on the faucet and let the water run. She wore a floral-printed dress and a pair of decorative sandals, looking soft and pretty, with her silky hair and pregnant glow. "Roberta seemed so sad last night."

"That's what I thought, too. But she didn't respect her son's wishes. She didn't cut me any slack."

"Then maybe you shouldn't care. Maybe you *should* let it go."

"That's what I keep telling myself. If Aaron's mother wants a relationship with him, then she should make the first move. She should fix what she helped destroy."

Carrie gave a brisk nod. "Exactly."

Talia blew out the pent-up air in her lungs. "Then why doesn't that make me feel better? Why can't I just listen to Aaron and let it go?"

Because he was hurting, she thought. And no matter what, he still loved his family.

Three uneventful days passed. No, Talia thought. Not uneventful. At least not emotionally.

She sat at her desk, looking out her office window. Her marriage was strained, riddled with what had become her husband's unspoken angst. Aaron was trying to put on a good show, but she knew he was a mess inside.

And so was she.

She pushed away the file in front of her, unable to concentrate on her job.

Twenty minutes passed, and then thirty. Finally she got up and went to Aaron's office, where she found him tapping at the keys on his computer.

He looked up at her and smiled. She returned his smile, but her effort was forced. He looked tired: rough, rugged and working-himself-to-the-bone strung out. His hair fell haphazardly over his forehead, and his tie was slightly askew. His jacket had been discarded hours ago; it lay in a heap on a leather chair.

"I can't do this any more," Talia said.

Panic edged his voice. "Do what?"

"Pretend everything is okay."

"With our marriage?" He stood up, and his shoulders blocked the artwork, a Salvdor Dali print, behind him.

"With us avoiding your family." She nearly wobbled on her shoes, feeling a bit dizzy, overwhelmed by the sudden decision she'd made. "I'm going to see your mom. Today." She glanced at the clock on the wall. "Now."

"Damn it, Tai. I told you—"

She held up her hand to stop his aggressive barrage. She needed all of the courage she could muster. "I don't want to be responsible for you losing you family. If I talk to your mom, then at least I did something. I tried to fix it."

"Yeah, and if she treats you badly, things will only get worse."

"I know." She reached for his Rolodex and opened it, searching for his mom's address. "But it's important to me to convince her that I love you. That our marriage wasn't a mistake."

He frowned at the address she jotted down. "Are you going to win my aunt over, too? My mom and my aunt live together. You can't approach one without the other."

Her pulse shimmied. "So I'll talk to both of them."

"Don't you see how pointless this is?"

"Why?" She shoved the address in her pocket. Talia was wearing her usual attire, a short skirt and a slim-fitting jacket. "Because you're too big and bad and macho to let your wife make things better?"

"Don't even go there." He loosened his skewed tie. "This isn't a contest. This is our lives."

"Yes, it is. And that's why I'm not going to let you stop me. I have to do this, Aaron."

He came around his desk and held onto her wrists. "What am I going to do with you?"

"Nothing." She pulled away from him. "Nothing but give me this chance."

"Do you want me to go with you?" he asked.

She studied him. "Do you want to go?"

His eyes flashed: dark, hard and stubborn. "No."

"Then don't. I can handle this on my own." When she walked away from him, she heard him curse.

She ignored the harsh, sexually vile word. All of the men at SPEC used it, lacing their dialogue with the expletive. Sometimes Talia used it, too.

Which wasn't a good selling point, she decided. Cursing like a sailor wouldn't endear her to Aaron's family.

Talia headed south on the freeway. Once she was out of the L.A. area, she sailed through the sporadic traffic and used a GPS to find her mother-in-law's house. She knew it was located near Aaron's tribal residence. Only now, Aaron didn't intend to spend any more time there. He didn't want anything to do with his Pechanga roots.

Thirty minutes later she parked in front of his mother's pristine home, a single-story structure that had been built after Aaron reached adulthood. With its bay-window flair and blue-and-white trim, it looked far too new to have been the house where he'd grown up. But that was common on this reservation. The recent success of the tribe had given its members the opportunity to improve their lifestyles.

Talia got out of her car, smoothed her skirt and hoped that Aaron's aunt didn't answer the door.

No such luck. She rang the bell, and Lynn appeared with a tight-lipped expression. She wore a standard gray sweat suit, and her hair was pulled away from her face, creating a stern, schoolmarm-type look. It didn't suit her normally colorful style.

"Well, well," Lynn said. "Look what the Porsche dragged in."

Talia lifted her chin. "Aaron and I have the same taste in cars."

"Where is my nephew?"

"He preferred to stay at the office."

"So you came alone." Lynn's expression remained tight. "My sister wanted to call Aaron, to apologize to him, but I talked her out of it."

"Why?" Talia's heart skipped a shake-rattle-and-roll beat. Her breath all but vibrated. "Why would you talk her out of it?"

"Because she still doesn't trust you, and that would only upset him even more."

Talia wasn't about to be scared off, even if the fear of failure cut like a knife. "May I see her?"

Lynn didn't respond. Instead, she made a clipped gesture, inviting Talia inside. "Roberta is in the backyard, working in the garden. I'll go get her."

"Thank-you." Talia looked around, where the living room reflected feminine décor. Fuzzy pillows and tiffany-style lamps enhanced soft colors and lightly printed fabrics.

A few minutes later, Roberta entered through the kitchen and walked into the living room carrying a straw sun-hat. Her clothes, a T-shirt and baggy jeans, were smudged with dirt. Lynn wasn't with her. She and Talia were alone.

Completely alone.

With clock-ticking silence humming between them.

"I don't know where to start," Talia said.

"How about with some lemonade?" Roberta responded, hanging her hat on a coat rack and doing her best to be polite, even if her telltale posture was tense.

"That would be nice." And hopefully less awkward. Talia noticed a slew of pictures featuring Danny on the wall. There were photographs of Aaron, as well. She suspected that at one time his wedding portrait with Jeannie had been framed, too.

Roberta served the lemonade in tall frosty glasses. Talia thanked her and took a sip, wetting her mouth.

"I really do love your son, Mrs. Trueno."

Roberta sat in a wingback chair. "I'm not comfortable with why you accepted his proposal. You wanted him to give up his heritage for you. To choose you over his family."

"Yes, I did." Talia spoke honestly. "But I was hurting over the past and I resented you and Lynn. When Aaron and I dated the first time, I wanted him to marry me, but he refused because he knew his family wouldn't approve." She paused, made her point. "Because I'm not Pechanga."

"He made a vow to his father, and we wanted to see him fulfill that vow, to marry someone who was part of our culture."

"And he did. He married Jeannie."

"Yes, but Aaron couldn't get you off of his mind. When he and Jeannie were going through the divorce, she told us how he purposely destroyed their marriage over you."

"Aaron told me the same thing, and I wasn't happy about him putting me in the middle of it. But Jeannie moved on, and so did Aaron. Lynn had no right to accuse me of being a home wrecker."

Roberta sighed. "Lynn and I had intended to behave properly at the party, to respect Aaron's wishes. But then Lynn saw you, and, well…"

Talia shifted in her seat. "Why did you keep quiet?"

"I wanted to stop you and Aaron from leaving. I wanted to speak up, to believe that you were being sincere. But I couldn't tell if you were being honest or if you were playing us for fools."

"But Aaron already told you that I was trying to win your acceptance. That I was embracing your culture. That Danny was teaching me your language."

"I didn't know what to think about that. What if you were conning Aaron? What if you were pretending to care, reeling him in until the day you got the ultimate revenge and walked out on him?" Roberta's eyes watered, making her blink, making her seem self-conscious. "I never meant to hurt my son. I just wanted to protect him." She paused, blinked again. "Do you think he'll ever forgive me?"

"Do you believe I'm being sincere?" Talia asked. "Do you trust me now?"

"Yes. And I'm sorry, so sorry I didn't you a chance."

"Then Aaron will forgive you."

Roberta's eyes kept watering. "If you didn't love him, you wouldn't be here. You wouldn't have put yourself in this position." She smiled a little. "Lynn and I aren't the easiest women to deal with."

"You're not so bad." Talia smiled, too. "I think it'll be a while before Lynn trusts me."

"My sister has never been in love. She doesn't know what it feels like. But she was there for me when I lost my husband. She moved in with me and helped me raise Aaron."

"I wish I could have known his father."

"I think you would have impressed him, coming here today, honoring his son. And calling me Mrs. Trueno." Roberta's teary eyes twinkled. "May I call you Mrs. Trueno, too?"

This time *Talia* almost cried; *her* eyes almost watered. For her that was the purest form of acceptance.

A warm and tender acknowledgement that she was truly Aaron's wife.

It took two weeks for Aaron to convince his aunt to have dinner with him, Talia, his mother and Danny.

So here they were, he and Aunt Lynn, standing back, watching the kitchen activity. His mom and Talia were experimenting with an Apache recipe. Danny was in the thick of it, sorting acorns.

"Don't you want to help?" Aaron asked his aunt.

"They look like they're doing all right without me."

"It'd be more fun if you got involved. If we both did." He reached for her hand and led her into the kitchen, where Talia and his mom were cooking venison.

The Apache recipe was new to all of them. But it was a good start, Aaron thought. In some small way, they were teaching Danny about his grandfather's people.

The boy glanced up. "Know what, Daddy? We can't use the acorns with little holes in them 'cause they have bugs."

"Oh, yeah?" He nudged his aunt toward the discarded acorns. "Are these the ones with bugs?"

"Yep." Danny grinned. "Do you and Auntie Lynn like bugs?"

"I should say not." Lynn ruffled Danny's hair. "Now scoot over and I'll help you sort them."

Talia turned around and smiled, and Aaron's heart reacted, melting like the mush the acorns would become. She was everything he'd ever wanted, everything he'd ever hoped to have. She'd healed the ache inside his soul, teaching him the meaning of forgiveness. His family had treated her poorly, yet she'd risen above it, giving them the benefit of the doubt, searching for the good in them.

"Is there anything for me to do?" he asked.

"You could kiss your wife," his mom responded, giving him permission to be happy, to show affection for the woman he'd married.

"This pretty little blonde?" He moved closer and swept her into his arms, nuzzling her cheek with his lips.

"Oh, good grief." His aunt snorted. "Is it necessary to encourage them?"

"I think it is." His mom winked at Talia, and Talia winked back.

Aaron wondered what the women were brewing, other than the food. He saw a secret in their eyes. "What's going on with you two?"

"We're going to the Swedish Cultural Center next week," Talia said, meeting his gaze and making his heart do the mush thing again.

Intrigued, he cocked his head. "You and my mom?"

"Yes. She thought it would be nice to learn about my heritage, too."

"Good grief," his aunt said again, but Aaron ignored her. She never liked to admit when she was wrong. Or when someone else was doing something right. Still, she was here, being part of the family and for now that was enough.

"What types of things are you going to do at the cultural center?" Aaron asked Talia.

"They have all sorts of activities," she responded, her voice bright and bubbly, like a toast of pink champagne. "Folk dancing lessons, Scandinavian interest groups, monthly breakfasts."

Aaron knew how much this meant to Talia, to her identity, to the memory of her own mother. He wanted to spin her around in a circle, to share her enthusiasm, but he kept his cool.

He looked at Danny. "What do you think, son? Do you think Grandma and Talia are going to be good folk dancers?"

"Heck, yeah. They already told me I could come and watch."

"Maybe I could watch, too. Or maybe I could dance with them." Aaron gave into temptation and gave his wife a little twirl. She laughed and kissed him sweetly on the mouth.

When they separated, he looked up and smiled at his mother. She returned his smile, and he thanked her in their native tongue, saying the words softly, quietly.

He was proud, so proud, of the people he loved.

After the evening ended and his family went home, Aaron and Talia tucked Danny into bed, reading to him from his favorite book. Once he nodded off, they walked to their own room.

"It was a perfect night, wasn't it?" Talia said, closing the door and making him long to hold her.

"Yes, it was. But it isn't over. Not yet." Aaron moved closer, inhaling the fragrance of her skin, filling himself with her scent, her radiance. "Lie down with me, Tai."

"Always." With her hair loose and falling beautifully across her shoulders, she heightened the romance, the quiet ambience.

He stepped back, and they removed their shoes and climbed into bed to cuddle, fully clothed and needing to wrap each other in intimacy.

Later they would make love. But for now, they wanted to share the tenderness brimming between them.

He shifted to look at her, to meet her gaze. "You're everything to me," he said. "Everything and more."

Her eyes turned watery. "It's been a long, painful road. But it was worth it." She paused, skimmed his jaw, tracing his features, the angles of his face. "You're worth it, Aaron. You always were."

He sucked in his breath, riveted by the power of her words, the familiarity of her touch. Their lives had come full circle. They'd blended their hearts, their souls, their worlds.

Completing each other in every way.

* * * * *

THE TRUENO BRIDES *trilogy concludes*
next month in Silhouette Desire.
Don't miss Sheri WhiteFeather's
THE MORNING-AFTER PROPOSAL,
available in October.

Set in darkness beyond the ordinary world.
Passionate tales of life and death.
With characters' lives ruled by laws the everyday
world can't begin to imagine.

Introducing NOCTURNE, *a spine-tingling new*
line from Silhouette Books.

The thrills and chills begin with
UNFORGIVEN by Lindsay McKenna

Plucked from the depths of hell, former military sharpshooter Reno Manchahi was hired by the government to kill a thief, but he had a mission of his own. Descended from a family of shape-shifters, Reno vowed to get the revenge he'd thirsted for all these years. But his mission went awry when his target turned out to be a powerful seductress, Magdalena Calen Hernandez, who risked everything to battle a potent evil. Suddenly, Reno had to transform himself into a true hero and fight the enemy that threatened them all. He had to become a Warrior for the Light….

Turn the page for a sneak preview of
UNFORGIVEN by Lindsay McKenna.
On sale September 26, wherever books are sold.

Chapter 1

One shot...one kill.

The sixteen-pound sledgehammer came down with such fierce power that the granite boulder shattered instantly. A spray of glittering mica exploded into the air and sparkled momentarily around the man who wielded the tool as if it were a weapon. Sweat ran in rivulets down Reno Manchahi's drawn, intense face. Naked from the waist up, the hot July sun beating down on his back, he hefted the sledgehammer skyward once more. Muscles in his thick forearms leaped and biceps bulged. Even his breath was focused on the boulder. In his mind's eye, he pictured Army General Robert Hampton's fleshy, arrogant fifty-year-old features on the rock's surface. Air exploded from between his lips as he brought the avenging hammer down. The boulder pulverized beneath his funneled hatred.

One shot...one kill...

Nostrils flaring, he inhaled the dank, humid heat and drew it deep into his massive lungs. Revenge allowed Reno to endure his imprisonment at a U.S. Navy brig near San Diego, California. Drops of sweat were flung in all directions as the crack of his sledgehammer claimed a third stone victim. Mouth taut, Reno moved to the next boulder.

The other prisoners in the stone yard gave him a wide berth. They always did. They instinctively felt his simmering hatred, the palpable revenge in his cinnamon-colored eyes, was more than skin-deep.

And they whispered he was different.

Reno enjoyed being a loner for good reason. He came from a medicine family of shape-shifters. But even this secret power had not protected him—or his family. His wife, Ilona, and his three-year-old daughter, Sarah, were dead. Murdered by Army General Hampton in their former home on USMC base in Camp Pendleton, California. Bitterness thrummed through Reno as he savagely pushed the toe of his scarred leather boot against several smaller pieces of gray granite that were in his way.

The sun beat down upon Manchahi's naked shoulders, grown dark red over time, shouting his half-Apache heritage. With his straight black hair grazing his thick shoulders, copper skin and broad face with high cheekbones, everyone knew he was Indian. When he'd first arrived at the brig, some of the prisoners taunted him and called him Geronimo. Something strange happened to Reno during his fight with the name-calling prisoners. Leaning down after he'd won the scuffle, he'd snarled into each of their bloodied faces that if they were going to call him anything, they would call him *gan,* which was the Apache word for *devil*.

His attackers had been shocked by the wounds on their faces, the deep claw marks. Reno recalled doubling his fist as they'd attacked him en masse. In that split second, he'd gone into an altered state of consciousness. In times of danger, he transformed into a jaguar. A deep, growling sound had emitted from his throat as he defended himself in the three-against-one fracas. It all happened so fast that he thought he had imagined it. He'd seen his hands morph into a forearm and paw, claws extended. The slashes left on the three men's faces after the fight told him he'd begun to shape-shift. A fist made bruises and swelling; not four perfect, deep claw marks. Stunned and anxious, he hid the knowledge of what else he was from these prisoners. Reno's only defense was to make all the prisoners so damned scared of him and remain a loner.

Alone. Yeah, he was alone, all right. The steel hammer swept downward with hellish ferocity. As the granite groaned in protest, Reno shut his eyes for just a moment. Sweat dripped off his nose and square chin.

Straightening, he wiped his furrowed, wet brow and looked into the pale blue sky. What got his attention was the startling cry of a red-tailed hawk as it flew over the brig yard. Squinting, he watched the bird. Reno could make out the rust-colored tail on the hawk. As a kid growing up on the Apache reservation in Arizona, Reno knew that all animals that appeared before him were messengers.

Brother, what message do you bring me? Reno knew one had to ask in order to receive. Allowing the sledgehammer to drop to his side, he concentrated on the hawk who wheeled in tightening circles above him.

Freedom! the hawk cried in return.

Reno shook his head, his black hair moving against his broad, thickset shoulders. *Freedom? No way, Brother. No way.* Figuring that he was making up the hawk's shrill message, Reno turned away. Back to his rocks. Back to picturing Hampton's smug face.

Freedom!

*Look for UNFORGIVEN by Lindsay McKenna,
the spine-tingling launch title
from Silhouette Nocturne™.*
Available September 26, wherever books are sold.

nocturne™

Save $1.⁰⁰ off

your purchase of any
Silhouette® Nocturne™ novel.

Receive $1.00 off
any Silhouette® Nocturne™ novel.

**Available wherever books are sold, including most
bookstores, supermarkets, drugstores and discount stores.**

Coupon expires December 1, 2006. Redeemable at participating
retail outlets in the U.S. only. Limit one coupon per customer.

RETAILER: Harlequin Enterprises Ltd. will pay the face value of this coupon plus
8¢ if submitted by the customer for this specified product only. Any other use
constitutes fraud. Coupon is nonassignable. Void if taxed, prohibited or restricted by
law. Void if copied. Consumer must pay for any government taxes. Mail to Harlequin
Enterprises Ltd., P.O. Box 880478, El Paso, TX 88588-0478, U.S.A. Cash value 1/100
cents. Limit one coupon per customer. Valid in the U.S. only.

5 65373 00076 2   (8100) 0 11265

SNCOUPUS

Silhouette

nocturne™

Save $1·00 off

your purchase of any
Silhouette® Nocturne™ novel.

Receive $1.00 off
any Silhouette® Nocturne™ novel.

Available wherever books are sold, including most bookstores, supermarkets, drugstores and discount stores.

Coupon expires December 1, 2006. Redeemable at participating retail outlets in Canada only. Limit one coupon per customer.

52607136

SNCOUPCDN

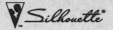

Silhouette Desire

COMING NEXT MONTH

#1753 FORBIDDEN MERGER—Emilie Rose
The Elliotts
When a business tycoon falls for the one woman he can't have, their secret affair threatens to stir up *more* than a few hot nights.

#1754 BLACKHAWK'S BETRAYAL—Barbara McCauley
Secrets!
Mixing business with pleasure was not on her agenda…but bedding the boss may be the key to discovering the truth about her family.

#1755 THE PART-TIME WIFE—Maureen Child
Secret Lives of Society Wives
A society wife learns her husband is leading a double life and gets whisked into his world of scandals and secrets.

**#1756 THE MORNING-AFTER PROPOSAL—
Sheri WhiteFeather**
The Trueno Brides
He vowed to protect her under one condition—she become his wife. Will she succumb to her desires and his zealous proposal?

#1757 REVENGE OF THE SECOND SON—Sara Orwig
The Wealthy Ransomes
This billionaire bets he can seduce his rival's stunning granddaughter, until the tables turn and *she* raises the stakes.

**#1758 THE BOSS'S CHRISTMAS SEDUCTION—
Yvonne Lindsay**
Sleeping with the boss she secretly loved was not the best career move. Now she had to tell him she was expecting his baby.